Mint Vinyl

James H. Wroe

Illustrated by Jordan Proctor

Copyright © 2023 by James Wroe

All rights reserved

Chapter 1

Uncle George

The silence of the empty house was suddenly broken by the half-hourly chiming of the long-case clock that stood in the hallway. The noise caused me to glance at my watch — it was 1:30pm, Friday the 20th of April 2012. I was standing by the window, looking out on what had started as quite a bright day, which had now been overtaken by a very abrupt seasonal shower. I could see the surrounding fields and trees, and an old-fashioned lamp post standing on the edge of a neat and pretty garden. The flowers that my Auntie Suzanne had planted were once again beginning to bloom.

On returning to the property, my mind was filled with wonderful thoughts and memories of the times I had spent there with both my auntie and uncle. Just one week earlier I had attended my Uncle George's funeral. A number of his friends had commented that 'Old Robbo' had had a good innings — a sentiment I had to agree with. Mr George Roberts was eighty-two when he passed away, though he was known to most by the nickname 'Robbo' — it was one of those things that stuck with him. There were also a few

Mint Vinyl

people who referred to him as 'Crazy George', as my uncle was rather eccentric.

I had come to the property on my uncle's request via his solicitor, a Mr J. Baxter—a local man well known to him. The house was number 14, Sycamore Lane, in the suburbs of Dansford—about fifteen miles southeast of Brenton in the Northwest of England. Earlier that morning I had received a phone call from old Mr Baxter asking if I would be so kind as to collect a letter addressed to me. Doing just that, I was given the letter by old Baxter himself with the instructions that I was to go to number 14 before opening the letter.

The rain—now streaking down the windowpanes—was obscuring my view out of the window. What was it all about? Why was I here? I found it all very intriguing, and more than a little mysterious.

Chapter 2

The Key

As I stood looking out of the widow, the rain was now beginning to clear, and gaps of blue sky were starting to appear. As so many thoughts had flooded my mind on returning to my uncle's house, I had almost forgotten the letter I was clutching in my hand. Having regained my thoughts, I sat down at the table and opened the letter. It was from my uncle, it read:

> *Dear Jack,*
>
> *Please find enclosed a key that I hope will help shape your future by bringing to fruition all of your long-held dreams that we spoke of so many times. Please go to the workshop where you will find a tall cabinet. Use the key to open the box that is in the bottom drawer of the cabinet.*

Once again, my mind began to race, not thinking of the past but of the future — my future. I was intrigued. Sure enough, I remembered many conversations with my uncle about my plans and dreams, part of which included a very great passion for collecting vinyl albums. I had become an avid collector, acquiring many of them through private sales and later via the internet. I had also begun to sell many online, but my real dream was to own my own record shop, selling as many mint condition albums as I could find. I had also decided that I would name my shop 'Mint Vinyl'.

Still sitting at the table my thoughts were like a blur. It felt as if my head was spinning. I Thought, *Just what could my uncle have in mind for me? Could it be money?* These thoughts were dismissed from my mind quickly, for at the reading of my uncle's will, I had already been bequeathed the sum of five thousand pounds, and the property had been left to my mother. The only way to find out was to go to my uncle's workshop, so I made my way to the rear of the house where the workshop lay.

With both excitement and trepidation, I entered the workshop, located the cabinet, and pulled open the bottom drawer, taking out a large steel safety box. Taking the key from my pocket, I opened the box. Inside, there were two envelopes both bearing my name. One of these envelopes had *'read first'* written on it. So, sitting down at the desk in the workshop, I took a letter opener, opened the envelope, and took out the letter. I took a deep breath and a short pause and started to read it. It read:

The Key

Jack,

I am sure that I don't have to remind you just how much you and your parents were loved by Suzanne and me, and how many happy and precious times we shared together. On reading this you may feel a little sad but cheer up son. We had a great life, and now your future offers great possibilities.

Uncle George then went on to relate how in many ways he had been a very private person, sometimes seeming very aloof, and that although he had never spoken of his work with the RAF, he now thought it was time.

It was for this very reason I was engaged in working on top-secret projects.

It was one of these projects that was about to blow my mind. Nothing could prepare me for the bombshell that was about to explode on me. My uncle explained that he, along with five other men — later joined by two very bright young ladies — were drafted in by the RAF to work on a very secret project. I was aware that my uncle was a very intelligent man, but until now I had simply failed to realise what a genius he really was. I was astounded by what I read. I read and re-read the letter several times, wondering whether it could really be true. It seemed that this group of highly in-

Mint Vinyl

telligent people had been brought together to work on the possibility of:

...*Time Travel.*

I was thinking after several readings — as most would — that these people must have been mad and had completely lost their senses. Of all the things I expected to read, I would never have come up with this. As I pondered further, my mind made various objections to it all. I thought, *They must have all been crackpots, lunatics, a few notes short of a bank.* Although, as I recalled, Uncle George was such a rational man — I began to think that there must be something in it after all.

> *So, you see my boy, the RAF wanted to acquire technology from the future regarding weapons, wanting them for the present time. This had all been set up in 1938 when it seemed to many that war was inevitable, so all of this would be of national importance.*

It seemed that they had worked for a number of years (not specified in the letter) without success. Then one day, after much failure, they made a sudden breakthrough. They had succeeded in making some kind of fracture or portal in time, although they could not be sure of the exact time and place the portal had opened to. Unfortunately, as soon as they had made this progress the fracture disappeared due to equipment failure. However, there was hope at the very least that they were in fact making progress. They worked hard to improve their equipment as best they could with the materials available to them. It wasn't financial restraint that held them back, but the available technology of the day. After a further month of work — and many sleepless nights — their supplier was able to acquire some new and experimental components, allowing them to get back on track.

> *Once again, we were able to make the fracture, but this time it appeared to remain stable — so far so good. What we observed was to become a characteristic of the function of the equipment. As we all looked out of the window of the laboratory, the scene before us became wavy and distorted — almost like looking at a heat haze in a hot country. Then, within a few seconds, it would appear normal again.*

The letter continued to explain the equipment in great detail, which I tried to simplify in my mind so I could understand it. There was a large radio-like device, with lots of dials and switches, and an oscilloscope screen. This device was in turn linked to another smaller device with dials for inputting the date and time. There was also a rather large pair of goggles containing a transmitter and receiver — a portable link to the equipment.

Mint Vinyl

Now that we had been able to get the fracture to remain stable (and refine our equipment to allow us to input a specific time) we could once again resume the experiment. However, every time we set the dial to a future date the fracture would suddenly collapse before us. This was a major problem for the project, bringing about many staff meetings where numerous varying views were expressed. Over a period of weeks, we tested the equipment over and over, yet every attempt at going into the future, be it one year or five years, was met with the same disappointing and frustrating outcome — failure. During one of the staff meetings, I suggested that we should set the equipment for a date in the past. I argued that we had tried the future without success, so we should try to determine if the equipment was indeed functioning correctly.

It was agreed that they should at least try, as progress had come to a complete standstill. Everything was made ready, and the dials set for one year in the past. They looked at the scene out of the window and there seemed to be no difference. They tried the experiment again, this time setting the dial back a further two years.

Suddenly the scene changed, the trees outside appeared smaller, and a building, presently complete

The Key

and occupied, was in the process of being built. A wave of excitement and exhilaration raced through all of the team.

Though they had seen that their device had indeed worked, it was pointed out by one team member that even though they had been successful in traveling to the past, their real objective was still eluding them.

The RAF didn't want to know what had already been, but what was to come, and know it in the present. After making a report to the committee for the RAF, we were individually asked of our opinions as to why the device had been unsuccessful in passing into the future. Varying ideas were put forward, some rather technical, and as such not easily understood by the committee.

However, my idea was much easier to understand. I simply believe that you can go into the past because it's there, it exists, but the future is different. Sure, with each day we are passing into it, but until then I don't believe that for us it is there. Needless to say, this was hotly disputed by most of my colleagues. It was finally decided that we would be given a further six months to try to resolve the problems — failure would result in the entire project being cancelled and shut down. After six months passed with no progress, the team was disbanded and set to work on other important projects, not quite so off the wall. The RAF made the final statement at the end of the project:

"There's no future in the past."

Uncle George was left with a dilemma. After all, the entire project had worked, in one direction at least.

Chapter 3

The Second Letter

I put down the letter on the desk. My head was still swimming from all that I had read. In fact, it felt like I was getting a dull headache, so I decided to take a break and make myself a brew. As I went to the kitchen and put the kettle on, a sudden thought about my Auntie Suzanne came to mind. Whenever I would say to her that I was putting the kettle on she would always reply, 'It won't fit you.' Funny how things are triggered off in your mind.

Having returned to the workshop, I sat down once more at the desk. What a day this was turning out to be. If Uncle George's friends had read his letter, they really would have called him 'Crazy George'. I must confess that I was still finding this whole thing somewhat difficult to come to terms with. After all, travelling in time is a mind-blowing thing. Trying to gather my thoughts again, I looked once more at the contents of the box I had opened. There was a second letter in there. I took it out to reveal some money in the bottom of the box. This was not the money I was used to using. There was in total: three one-pound notes, two ten-shilling notes, three half crowns, five shillings, and a sixpence. At that precise moment it hadn't crossed my mind why my uncle would have placed this money in the box. With all the events of the day I must admit that I hadn't joined up the dots. I was blissfully unaware of Uncle George's intentions for me. Having placed the money back into the box, I took hold of the second letter. Once again it was worded *Mr Jack Roberts*, along with the words '<u>most important</u>'. Obviously, the letter had to be opened, but at that moment I was filled not only with excitement at what it might contain, but also some trepidation. For the first time, I really began to think about what my uncle's intentions for me might be.

    I sat for a few moments, trying desperately to gather my thoughts to some sort of normality. I doubted if that was even possible anymore. By now the pressure over my eyes was quite severe, my headache having grown much worse. I looked at my watch, it was now 5:30pm. Just where had the time gone? I suppose having had nothing to eat since breakfast that morning was not helping the situation. As I stared down at the unopened letter, the word on the envelope became blurred. As much as I wanted to open it, I just couldn't concentrate. It was just no good, I would have to go home, get something to eat, and hopefully get some rest. I put the two letters back into the box, took out the key from my pocket, locked the box, and put it back into the bottom drawer of the tall cabinet. I made my way out, locking up

The Second Letter

behind me and thinking to myself, *tomorrow I will return, hopefully feeling much better.*

I don't recall the journey home other than calling into the local chippy and getting some chips and gravy. Getting back in, I made myself a brew and sat down to eat my chips and gravy. I found myself just picking at it, and eventually I just left it. Having taken something for my now pounding headache, I decided to go to bed. At around 8pm I drifted off to sleep quite quickly. My rest would not last too long as I woke up abruptly and, glancing at my clock, saw that it was now 10:15pm. I lay there wide awake. My mind was just full of the events of the day. The rest of the night passed this same way — a little sleep, then my pondering thoughts would return. Once again, I turned towards the clock. It was now 4:30am on Saturday morning. I couldn't wait any longer, I would have to open that second letter. I got up, showered, got dressed, and returned to Uncle George's house.

I recall the journey to number 14 quite clearly. Because it was still early in the morning, I only saw one person, a milkman. He was far too busy to take any notice of me and we passed each other like ships in the night. I arrived at number 14 and took out my key, letting myself in and feeling a very real sense of excitement. I went straight to the workshop, took out the box from the tall cabinet, and lay it on the desk and opened it. I gazed at the letter before me on the desk. Suddenly my mind was telling me that, once again, I was not looking after myself. I had rushed out of my place without any breakfast, but it was too late now, I had to know what Uncle George had written to me. Finally, I took the letter opener and opened the letter. It read:

My Dearest Jack

I don't have to remind you of the closeness of the three of us, and of the way we have sought to realise your dreams and aspirations. I know that, in these last twelve months or so, I have not been myself. But losing my darling Su was almost too much to bear. I know that you will find it in your heart to forgive me.

At this point tears flowed down my cheeks. I was reminded of how it felt to lose my precious auntie, and the wonderful love she had for Uncle George and myself. The letter continued:

I know how you were upset by these things, both the loss of Auntie Suzanne and the way in which it affected me. I am so sorry that I must have seemed so distant, she was just so special to me. Anyway, back to you, Jack, we always wanted you to realise your dream of owning a record shop. You have achieved this goal in a small way with your private sales and your internet site, however you were always hampered by the supply of mint conditions albums. Well,

The Second Letter

> *I believe that we can, between us, do something about this difficulty. I know that the money I left to you will go some way to help, but the real difference will come from my research. When the RAF project was disbanded, the thought occurred to me that it might be both useful and interesting to go back in time. So, I set up my workshop at home to do that very thing. Over quite a long period of time, I was able to improve on our initial apparatus, knowing that advances would be made in the field of electronics. My dear Jack, I am so pleased to tell you that things have gone extremely well. I feel that you will indeed be impressed by my progress. Now, before you read on I propose you just ponder for a short while what you have read so far.*

Taking Uncle George's advice, I went to make myself a brew and found some biscuits that were still okay to eat. After a very much needed drink and food, I returned to the letter. I read on:

> *Now, these next things are very important so take them to heart, they are instructions on how to use the, for want of a better term, 'time machine'. Jack, my boy, what I am proposing to you is that you travel back in time to get the mint vinyl albums that you need for your store. The money in the box should be*

Mint Vinyl

able to provide your first one. Just think, Jack, the fulfilment of that long held dream.

Once again, my head was swimming, I could hardly believe it myself, it was just so overwhelming. My mind raced as I thought of all the possibilities all this could bring. 'Mint Vinyl' could be a reality. I read on, Uncle George explaining the equipment to me:

Right on top of the tall cabinet there is an old-fashioned radio.

I looked over to the tall cabinet and sure enough there it was. It was quite large, in a polished wooden cabinet, it really did look old. You wouldn't give it a second glance if you didn't know what it was all about. Next, he gave me the instructions for turning it on. *How hard could it be*, I thought. I read on:

Use the switch on the far right, turn to your right.

I turned the switch and the radio burst into life, I was surprised as music came out of it. Slightly confused I began to read again:

Bet that had you fooled, but that's the whole point. It has been designed to fool anyone who should happen

The Second Letter

to turn it on. Next, turn the same switch to the left and then right again.

Having followed these instructions, the dial suddenly changed from a dull yellowish glow to a bright red. I again read on:

Now flick down the switch on the far left.

I flicked the far-left switch, and, to my surprise, a drawer came out from the bottom left of the radio. I certainly wasn't expecting that. Inside the drawer was a dark blue spectacles case, really quite ordinary looking. Inside was a pair of spectacles, nice but not fancy or the designer type of thing you see today. Then the instructions read:

Now flick the switch up, then back to the middle.

This being done, the drawer door shut up and a little blue light above the switch went out. I guessed from reading the first letter that the specs were the link between the radio part of the equipment, although I wondered how as they looked for all the world like a normal, very ordinary pair of spectacles. I could see nothing that would lead me to suppose anything to the contrary. I returned once more to this second letter. I must admit I was beginning to feel somewhat bemused by the whole thing. Anyway, I read on:

Mint Vinyl

> *Though they don't look it, these spectacles are like no others you have ever seen. Put them on Jack and take a look at yourself in the mirror on the wall.*

Intrigued, I put on the spectacles, got up from the desk, and walked over to the mirror on the wall. To my absolute amazement there appeared to be no spectacles on my face, I could not believe what was happening. Uncle was right, these spectacles were like no others I had seen.

> *I have designed them this way so if you don't normally wear glasses then you can't see them, and they will just become plain lenses. If on the other hand you do wear glasses, they will become whatever prescription lens you require.*

Just as I was coming to terms with this, the letter went on:

> *Now touch the top of the rims with a finger of each hand simultaneously.*

I carried out this instruction, what happened next absolutely startled me, almost causing me to reel backwards. Suddenly, right in front of my eyes was a multi coloured touch screen display kind of like in the movies. I was just gobsmacked for want of a better phrase. On my left was a display showing the present date and time displayed in blue. In the middle was another display in green which

The Second Letter

read: 'dates in time', time starting at the current date—by scrolling, any date required could be selected. Finally, on the right there was display in red which showed the days of the week and the time of day. Uncle George had said that these spectacles were like no others, and he was right, these specs were without a doubt the coolest things I had ever seen in my life. I was elated and excited but all a little light-headed. I really felt that I should share this with someone, but I knew that it would be impossible. I took off the spectacles and returned them to their case. They appeared visible again, it was truly remarkable. I looked down once more at Uncle George's letter, there was still some more to be read. Once again, a feeling of euphoria hit me, my mind was racing and I was physically shaking, I knew that I needed to take a break and get some fresh air.

I made my way outside and, just as I got to the front garden, a neighbour was passing by walking his dog, Patch. He was a neighbour but not the next-door kind, for he lived a good thirty-minute walk from my uncle's house on the Firsgrove Estate. Reg Burrows was his name, a good friend of my uncle. He asked how I was doing and whether I was putting things in order at Uncle George's house. I said that I was fine and that I was just sorting out a few things. I longed to share my discoveries, but of course I did no such thing. I knew that I must put away these thoughts, though I admit that after seeing all those things, it would have been good to share with someone. I took a deep breath and, having pulled myself together, went inside and made myself a brew. Once again, I had not eaten for a good period of time. Ever since these recent events, my world had been turned completely upside down. Once again, I took out the letter, sat at the desk and began to read once more:

> *There are a few things that you need to know about going into the past. Take my advice Jack, don't rush headlong into this, you must make proper preparations for what you are about to embark on. I know that you will be excited, believe me boy I was too, but the first thing to tell you is that I now have full confidence in my apparatus. You see right from the early days with the RAF there was always a problem keeping the fracture stable. After a very long time, I was able to figure out what was going wrong, and with advances in technology all has been able to be fixed. Now, when you switch the radio on and put on the spectacles and activate them, just reach out with your finger to the displays and set them to your requirement. This done, you will notice a bright circle at the bottom of the display. Just touch it and away you go. You will then see what will become very familiar to you, the scene before you will become wavy and distorted, then it will stabilise after a matter of seconds. This is just the machine making the fracture so you can pass into the past. Whenever you are ready just*

The Second Letter

> *step forward into the past. Forward into the past, has a nice ring to it don't you think Jack my boy? May I suggest that you don't do it at this moment, for I must relay to you some other things. When you step into the past you may feel dizzy or light-headed, or even quite nauseated. With me, I felt light-headed and a little sick, but you will just have to see what happens to you Jack. The machine will let you go to another time, but not to another place. Wherever you are in the present, you will arrive there in the past. This will also apply, in reverse, to the return journey. In order to travel back to the present, you must be within three miles of the machine's present location. This must be considered when you make your preparations.*

Thinking about this made me consider that it might be better to take the machine to my place, a top-floor apartment at the quayside. A sudden fear struck my mind, just how could I walk into the past from up there. It would be the death of me. I need not have worried about my health, for having read on in my uncle's letter, he explained to me some things which now seem fairly obvious.

> *Some things that exist in the future, may not exist in the past, but there's no need to worry, as the equipment has been configured to make sure that you will*

always step onto solid ground when you take a step forward into the past.

By default, when you wish to return to your own time, the displays will be set to return you to the exact moment you left. As a result, you technically will be in the past yourself, given that time will naturally elapse while you are away. Otherwise, you can manually set the display to the exact time you would like to return to. For your ease, I have ensured that the display cannot be set beyond the limits of the present, so, when you want to return from the past, you can easily set the display to let the maximum possible time elapse.

Chapter 4

A Glimpse into the Past

Having read the letter in full, I lay it down on the desk, thinking about the immensity of the facts that I had come in possession of. I could not decide whether I was happy, confused, or a little bit mad. In fact, I was really all of these things, but all I really knew for sure is that my life could never be the same again. As much as I longed to see if all these things were indeed true, Uncle George was absolutely right — this undertaking would require a lot of preparation. I knew I would need to draw up a plan of action for the future, or was it for the past? I smiled to myself as I thought that it was actually both — how many other people could say that? The first thing I needed to do was to bring back some kind of semblance to my life; I needed to get back to looking after myself. I looked at my watch — it was already 2:45pm on Saturday afternoon.

    I decided that I needed to return home and try to settle back into my life, at least some part of it. I returned the second letter to the steel box, locked it, and placed it back into the tall cabinet. I decided to lock up the workshop while I

Mint Vinyl

was away. I knew Uncle George had a key somewhere because sometimes I would find it locked while he was still alive. I looked around the workshop, and sure enough on a hook on the wall was a key ring with a leather fob embossed with an RAF symbol. *This must be it*, I thought, I walked to the door, taking one last look inside and then locked up the workshop.

Going back into the house, I made sure all was okay, then I left for home, locking up behind myself. I made my way down the garden driveway to the tall brick archway with a glossy black gate, with the number 14 in white close to the top of it. Surrounding the garden was a beautifully weathered fence that had stood the test of time, well maintained by my uncle. I made my way down the road, actually more of a wide path leading towards the Firsgrove Estate. Whilst walking through the estate, I came across several people who were known to me. Having exchanged hellos, and a few brief words, I continued on my journey home. There were a good number of children busily playing in the streets on what had become a very pleasant afternoon.

Having made my way home, I let myself into my apartment, took off my jacket and threw it on a chair. Then, slumping onto my sofa, I reached for the remote and switched on the television. I just stared at it, almost like you would a goldfish bowl. I just felt completely exhausted. I must have dozed off, as when I woke up it was early evening. There was some game show on the TV. I reached for the

A Glimpse into the Past

remote which had fallen off the sofa and turned it off, thinking I could do without that. Rubbing my eyes, I got up from the sofa thinking, *I must get something to eat.*

Going into my kitchen, I opened the fridge, taking out some mince I had in there. I then went to the veg rack, picked up an onion and got some rice out of the cupboard. I decided that if I had a jar of curry sauce it would be curry and rice for me. Thankfully there was a jar in the cupboard. After having a very welcome meal, for which I felt much the better for, I then decided I would need a notepad to formulate my plan of action. I searched in the drawers and cupboards of my apartment, finding nothing, except a very small jot pad, which was not of much use. *Off to the shops*, I thought to myself. I walked to the nearest shops, there are a good selection of shops at the Quayside and a couple of supermarkets — one large, the other more like a convenience store. By this time almost all the shops had closed, so I headed to the supermarket. I went in and got myself a basket, got some milk, remembering that I needed some after checking the fridge, a small loaf of bread, an A4 pad and a packet of three ball point pens.

Back at my place, I began with priority number one: putting the kettle on for a brew. Taking my drink into the lounge I sat on the sofa wondering what needed to be done. I took my pen and note pad and placed them on the coffee table. Opening to the first page of the notepad, I wrote 'Action Plan' as my heading. I quickly decided that my first excursions into the past would be brief—a kind of experiment to see how things went, mostly how it would affect me physically. After all I would be a total stranger, like a fish out of water. I decided to initially make two trips, to 1953 and 1926. I now needed to know something about these time periods, so some research at the local library and on the internet was my next step. As I was not planning on staying long on these trips, I saw no need of taking any money, but I did think it necessary to at least try and find some appropriate clothing. I had the idea of visiting some charity shops, as people donate all kinds of discarded clothing and footwear. I searched online, looking at information about the two time periods. As the next day was Sunday, part of my plan would have to wait. I would visit the library after work on Monday. The plan of action had begun, but I knew it would take much more research, I had only begun to scratch the surface really. It was beginning to get late, so I decided to go to bed setting my alarm for the usual 6:45am.

After showering and eating breakfast on Sunday morning, I made my way down to the car park outside. I got into my car, a Rover 3.5 litre, a big old saloon car in brilliant condition—and I must admit a bit of an indulgence—and sat reflecting on recent events. Once again, I had had a very disturbed sleep, lying there for what seemed like hours, unable to sleep. So much was going through my mind. After driving to work, a journey of about twenty minutes, I arrived at

A Glimpse into the Past

the company car park. I showed my pass to the security guard, and he in turn opened the barrier. I parked up with a few minutes left before I needed to go in and told myself I needed to get back into my routine. But the thought of being at work as opposed to being in the past was already seeming a real imposition. The company I was working for was a medium sized electronics company 'CAV', which stands for communications audio visual. My position at the time was in development and design, but I'm really a sort of guy who likes to get his hands dirty so to speak — I just like to be hands on. I just enjoyed my work, and wasn't interested in promotion, or at least I used to, I just didn't know anymore.

My working week passed over almost like I was in some kind of dreamworld. My days were spent at work, but my nights by contrast were spent with a longing to fulfil my plans and dreams. I surfed the net researching each night until Saturday finally arrived. I got up early on Saturday morning to make plans, finally deciding to visit several charity shops and even a jumble sale being held in a local church. Things went really well, and I managed to pick up some clothing and footwear appropriate for my trips.

Later, I sat on the sofa in my apartment with my purchases. I must say I was rather pleased with my progress — things were really starting to come together. A smile spread across my face as I suddenly thought of that American TV show with the guy who says, 'I love it when a plan comes together', and I must confess I do. Then I told myself I really needed to deal with what had become the really mundane part of my life. When I had to be at work and relate to other people, I needed to begin to be normal. I was already beginning to feel the benefits of eating both well and regularly again. It had been a full week since I was last at number 14.

After a much-needed good night's sleep, I got up ready to head to my uncle's house to transfer the equipment to my apartment. For the first time in a while, I had in fact managed to sleep well, and was up and ready for the task at hand. That Sunday morning was a little overcast, but I didn't mind, I knew it was going to be a great day come what may. I usually walked to my uncle's, but this time I drove there in order to transfer the machine. Arriving, I parked in the drive and made my way in, going straight to the workshop. All was how I had left it, I quickly unplugged the radio, taking it straight to the car and putting it safely in the boot. Returning, I got the steel box from the tall cabinet, locking everything up and putting the box on the front passenger seat of the car. I then got into the car and began my homeward journey.

I don't remember much about the journey home; I was preoccupied with thoughts of future journeys into the past. Getting back, I parked up, got the radio and the box, and took the lift up to my apartment. Once inside I placed the steel box on the coffee table and the radio on a long and sleek black cabinet — a stylish piece of modern furniture —

A Glimpse into the Past

yet the old radio somehow didn't look out of place sat on top. Sitting on the sofa for a few minutes I gathered my thoughts and made my way to the bedroom. I opened the wardrobe and took out the clothes I had chosen for the journey and got dressed in the somewhat old and rather tatty clothes and boots I had chosen. It was time for my first glimpse into the past. I had chosen 1926 for my first trip. Following my uncle's instructions, I turned on the radio at the plug. I turned the switch on the radio first to the right, then the left, and to the right again causing the dial to glow red. I then flicked the switch on the far left up, and out came the drawer with the spectacles. My heart began to beat faster, my pulse must have been racing. I put on the spectacles and touched the rims with two fingers, one on each side. The multi-coloured display was there before my eyes. I reached out my finger, moving each of the settings to the right place. All was set for 9:30am on the 14th of July 1926, this being a weekday, Wednesday to be precise. With my heart now feeling like it was in my mouth, I now touched the centre white circle.

Suddenly the view out of my window began to shimmer and waver, just like some kind of heat haze, everything appeared distorted. As suddenly as it had begun, it became completely stable. Immediately, I saw a vast change in my view, there was now a big open space before me. Fields with a row of what looked like stone cottages now appeared before me. I walked forward, and to my amazement I didn't

Mint Vinyl

fall from the top floor but found myself standing on the canal towpath. It was just amazing; in the heat of the moment, I had forgotten about how travelling to the past might make me feel. I became quite dizzy and more than a little disorientated. Suddenly, a man dressed in brown overalls, a leather apron, a jacket, and a flat cap spoke to me. "Are you alright, guv?" he asked. Startled by the man, I was now feeling better, coming quickly to my senses.

I quickly replied, "Yes I'm fine, thank you, my good man."

He replied, "You looked a bit shaken up there, guv. If you're sure yer alright, then I'll be getting back to work." The man had with him a two-wheeled truck, with what looked like a bale on it. It was covered with some kind of cloth. He raised his cap to me and said, "I'll be going then."

He went quickly towards the location of a big warehouse. It was just to the right of where my apartment block had been, or rather would be. Now, feeling much more myself, I started to look around me. It was a huge hive of activity; workmen like the one who had spoken to me were going to and fro from the warehouse. Some had two-wheeled trucks, some four, they were unloading barges on the canal, which was still there in my time, although everything appeared so different now There were two other barges waiting to come through the lock. On the towpath stood the lock keeper's house, only small but rather pretty. It was already a lovely day, even for early morning, everyone I saw was fresh faced

A Glimpse into the Past

and just seemed happy and the air smelt sweet and fresh. In the distance I could see more cottages, I presumed that these houses were for some of the workmen and their families. I could see women too near the cottages, hanging out washing and chatting to each other. There were also some farm buildings in the distance, and I could see some sheep in the fields and hear dogs barking. I noticed such a sharp difference between what I was seeing now and what I had left. Everything looked at peace.

Over to the left of where I stood, I could clearly see off in the distance what appeared to be the village. I saw the smoke billowing from the chimneys as I walked over the bridge which crossed the canal. As I continued walking, I was pulled up by a man just outside of the village. "Why are you not working today, my good fellow?" he asked. He was a stout man in his forties I'd say, wearing a suit and tie and a bowler hat. "Plenty of work at the warehouse if you're wanting work. Just ask for me — Smethurst, Mr Jack."

I replied, "Thank you for your generous offer, sir. I shall give it close consideration."

"Very well," he said, "good day to you, sir." After speaking to Mr Jack, I began to think that I must be getting back home. I made my way back to the towpath where I had first stood, and once again touching the rims of my spectacles I was presented with the touch screen. I reset the display and pressed the centre white circle. I then stepped forward, in an instant I observed the process and then I was back. It was truly an amazing day, but for now I was back in the present. The display had reset to the exact same time I had left, I hadn't lost any of the day. No time had progressed in the present while I was away. *How fantastic*, I thought to myself, knowing I could not tell another living soul, although I did doubt that anybody would believe me even if I did.

I got changed, putting back my clothes and boots in my wardrobe. I sat down to reflect on my trip, which all in all had gone really well. The whole thing was just astonishing. I decided I would celebrate by having a nice big tot of rum. I spent some time afterwards just going over in my mind about all that had happened. I then began to consider that interaction with people could be dangerous, but not entirely avoidable if was to go into the past.

I went to the kitchen and prepared myself a meal, then sat down and tried to watch the telly. I just couldn't seem to concentrate on the now anymore — now that the past was at my fingertips so to speak. After a while, I went to bed, once more sleeping fitfully. The next morning was the rat race once again. I was back at work again, trying to be more myself otherwise people there may have started to ask all sorts of awkward questions and I really didn't want that. While at work, I decided I would make the other trip to 1953 that day. I had done all of my preparations, found a nice suit, shirt, and tie, some very nice shoes, and even a hat for myself.

A Glimpse into the Past

I arrived home and changed into my 1950s clothes and looked in the mirror—very smart indeed. This time I decided to take some of the money Uncle George had put in the box for me. I was ready and excited, almost to the point of laughing out loud. I knew that this was just going to be brilliant. This time I had a mind to try and purchase my first mint vinyl, an album of the era. I went into the lounge, switched on the radio, flicked the switch for the specs, and set the display for 10am on the 2nd of June 1953. I touched the centre white disc, and away I went with the now familiar process. Before stepping forward, I looked at the scene before me. I looked towards the spot where the warehouse stood in 1929, it was no longer there. A large factory stood in its place, and although the canal was still there it was no longer busy with all the barges.

I stepped forwards once again and found myself standing on the canal tow path, but what a difference met my vision this time. It was hard to take it all in. There were lots and lots of terraced houses, narrow streets in every direction. There were also several major roads and, where the villages once stood, there was now a town. There were a number of people walking along the towpath, no doubt enjoying a morning stroll. A few people nodded to me as they walked by. I walked over the bridge towards a main road that I could see. As I got closer, I was intrigued by the sheer number of people lining both sides of the road.

Mint Vinyl

There were hundreds of people, and in the distance I could hear a brass band playing. As I got closer I saw lots of bunting everywhere, hundreds of Union flags were flying. People were jostling and there was lots of noise. Finally, I had to ask someone just what was going on, so I asked a man who was close by. He was wearing a very well-worn suit but seemed a pleasant enough guy. "Blimey," he replied, "where have you been hiding, mate? It's the Queen's coronation — everybody knows that."

What a wonderful day I had chosen for my trip, the atmosphere was electric. I just stood and watched the parade. In almost every street there were tables and chairs set up for street parties. The people were so joyous, which very easily rubbed off on me. I knew I would remember this day for a very long time to come. After about an hour or so I decided to try and find a record shop. After all, I had planned to find my first album. After picking my way through the crowds I came to a street called Firth Street, with a record shop on the corner called 'Robinson Records'. I opened the door and a little bell at the top of the door rang out. A man appeared from out back. "Can I help you, sir?" the man asked.

"Will it be okay if I just have a look around?" I asked.

"That's fine, sir," he answered, "take your time." I looked at the various records, which to be honest weren't very many. Not finding anything I really wanted to purchase, I went over to the counter to talk to the man.

A Glimpse into the Past

"Jack's the name, Jack Roberts. I'm just visiting town today. And you are?"

"Forgive me," he said, "I'm Peter Robinson the owner."

"I'm looking to start a record collection, but I can't seem to find anything. Is this all you have?" I asked.

"Well, I do have one more, sent by a friend from the States you know."

"Oh yes, who is it?"

"Frank Sinatra"

"Is it for sale?"

"It could be, but it will have to be twelve and six."

I put my hand in my pocket and took out some money, a ten-shilling note and a half crown, making twelve shillings and sixpence. I handed the money over to Peter and thanked him for all his help and made my way out of the shop. I closed the door behind me, my mind still on my first mint vinyl, it being one of the first of the new 33RPM.

I turned to walk back down the street when I bumped into a young guy with three of his mates. Right away from my research I knew that these were Teddy Boys. "Steady on there, pops," he said, "what's the big rush?" Grabbing me by the shoulders he continued, "Nice threads, pops." His mates nodded in agreement. Looking at the album I had bought, he took it from my hands. I didn't resist, not thinking it wise. "Well look here, Ol' Blue Eyes, hey, big daddy," he said.

41

Mint Vinyl

To which another replied, "Bad news. So, you like old Frankie baby then, pops?"

"Yes, I do," I answered.

"Well get with it, we don't see," he replied. They then proceeded to push me from one to the other. But just as they had started, apparently losing interest, they stopped.

"Nice bash eh, big daddy?" the first guy said, looking at the crowds. All four of them walked away leaving me with my album intact, I was very grateful for that.

"Later, gator," one of them shouted as he walked away, smiled, and turned around again.

Well, the day had not been quite what I had expected, but at least I was in one piece and that was good. I walked back to the towpath, and, finding myself alone, I prepared to go back home. I reached into my inside jacket pocket to get my notepad in which I had now written down two columns with dates and times for past and present so I would know exactly when to go back, should the automatic reset fail. In a moment I was back in my lounge in the present.

Chapter 5

The Swinging Sixties

My plans for the next trips into the past were now well underway. I had taken a couple of days holiday from work in order to do more research. I needed more currency of the relevant time periods—I had the little that Uncle George had provided but whatever else I could lay my hands on would surely be most welcome. I continued to surf the net, building up a catalogue of records that I thought most people would be interested in. I had attended some collectors shows, where I had picked up some cash. Not exactly what I would describe as a bank, but nonetheless still very helpful. I was also intending to search around some coin shops that I had been looking up. My wardrobe of period clothes was now beginning to grow considerably. I couldn't be seen in the same clothes all the time. I felt that I had to be fitting in, as though I was a real part of things.

At this point I was thinking, *When I return to work, I really must be normal in the present*, however difficult this was going to be, having worked really hard in my two days off. When it was time for my return to work, I felt like I could

Mint Vinyl

easily spend a week in bed. I felt reasonably satisfied with the way my two trips into the past had gone — even if the one into the fifties had had some difficulties with the Teddy boys. But overall, I didn't think about them with too much concern, they had only been a kind of experiment to get me used to travelling into the past. Even with the incident in the fifties I had been able to purchase my first album. I had now placed the album, *In the Wee Small Hours* by Frank Sinatra, into my collection.

I had a large record collection but possessed very few that were anywhere near mint condition. My music was a very real passion and a kind of retreat for me. It was a real part of my plans and dreams. Anyway, it was now time for me to go to bed for tomorrow it would be back to work. Thankfully I had started to sleep quite normally again. Before leaving for work I took from the wardrobe the outfit I would wear for my trip into the sixties. I must admit that it captured my mind for most of the day. Even though this had been the case I thought that I had coped quite well and had been very normal. At least it seemed that way to me, everyone just relating to me in the same old way. At last, it was time to return home. After taking a shower I prepared a meal and got dressed. I was now ready for my first trip into the swinging sixties. Coming into my lounge, I took a deep breath. I then thought to myself, *Have I got everything, wallet, change in my pockets, note pad and pen in my inside pocket?* I had already made a note of the times and dates etc. All was

The Swinging Sixties

well, so I turned on the radio, got the specs and putting them on I went through the procedure.

In a short space of time, I could now see the 1960s through my window, having chosen 1963. What a difference had taken place since the fifties. As I stood on the canal towpath there were now some council houses where my present apartment stood. As I looked around, I saw that quite a lot of the terraced houses of the fifties had been replaced by council houses as well as what I perceived to be semi-detached private houses—overall, a very different feel from the early fifties. To my right, the cotton mill was now occupied by a number of businesses rather than being used for its original function. From what I could see from a big board there was now a shoe manufacturer on two floors, a cloth manufacturer on the first floor, and a maker of gardening implements on the top floor—how times had changed. I had set the displays for the 1st of May 1963 at 11:30am. Once again, I am pleased to say, on my arrival there was already the beginning of a very fine day. The sun was shining, and the birds were singing so to speak. I made my way to my left, over the canal bridge. With no barges now on the canal, the canal looked quite derelict, and the lock keeper's house was in ruins. A number of people were walking on the footpath, mostly young people. Walking over the bridge, I could see the town, which had once again been changed. There were lots more houses than before and the roads were a little busier—more cars, lorries, and buses going up and down the main roads. Whenever I passed anyone, I smiled and said, "Good morning." People on the whole replied to me, which at least made me feel a little more comfortable. I walked down one of the main streets called Thomas Street. I looked around intently to see if I could find a record shop. I was also looking for a bookmakers. During my planning I came up with an idea to help with my need for funds of the day. I decided I would use the money I already had to place some bets to win some money. After all, I was at a unique advantage as I could get winners straight from the horse's mouth if you know what I mean. I could easily know the winners of any horse races and, as long as I didn't go mad, I could easily get some funds to purchase my records. Well at least that was my plan anyway. However, what is it they say about the best laid plans?

Walking along Thomas Street I came to the junction of Clifton Road. There, on the corner, was my bookies. The sign read, 'D. Rossi Turf Accountant'. *Here is my cash cow*, I thought to myself. Little did I know what I was letting myself in for. I would come to know Mr Rossi and his associates very well in the coming days. Going in, I was greeted by two guys behind the counter that I would later know as Mark Stanley and Robert Brown. These two men knew little of their employer's, shall we say, darker side. Having made myself known I went to the counter along the back wall. Finding betting slips and a small blue pen opposite the main counter, I took out my note pad and looked up today's rac-

The Swinging Sixties

ing. I made two bets at Kempton: the two o'clock and two-thirty races. Having placed my bets, I was about to leave when Dave Rossi himself came through the door — my very first sight of him. I must confess to not getting a good feeling about our Mr Rossi. I would say Dave was about 6 foot 4 inches tall. He was a well-built guy with chiselled features and a face well lived in — not what you might call friendly. I didn't know it at the time, but my suspicions of Mr Rossi were to be proven well founded. As well as owning the betting shop, Dave was also a money lender and, like most of his family, was what you might call a crook, having his fingers in lots of pies. Just before I left the shop I overheard Dave Rossi talking to Mark Stanley.

"Who was that guy? Haven't seen him in here before, or anywhere else for that matter," he said.

I closed the door behind me and carried on my journey. By now there were a good number of people on Thomas Street, some teenagers, and a lot of women busily going to the local shops along the high street. You name it and you could buy it along here. There were plenty of well stocked shops, I even saw some young lads (about ten or twelve years old) banging on a shop window of a grocer who had put up a display of canned foods a little too close to the window. They had banged so hard on the window that they sent the cans tumbling down. He wasn't very impressed to say the least. The boys quickly ran off, laughing as they did.

Mint Vinyl

I continued my search for a record shop. It was then that I came to the corner of Hunt Street and Den Street off Thomas Street. This was not, I thought, the best of locations, but the shop made up for this with a bright colourful sign above the window. It read 'Hibbert's Records', which was also written on the door. There was also a sign hanging on the back of the door saying: 'Welcome please come in'. The shop was very well lit and welcoming with various album covers visible in the window. *This looks very promising*, I thought to myself. Little did I know then that the owner of this shop would become a firm friend of mine and would be very influential in my life. I walked into the shop and was immediately impressed by the set up and by the warm welcome I received from both the man and the teenage girl behind the serving counter. I thanked them for their welcome, telling them I was new in the area and gave them my name. The guy immediately said, "Pleased to meet you, Jack, how are you, well I hope?" He then introduced himself and his seventeen-year-old daughter Lucy Hibbert. Lucy was a very pretty girl, very polite, and helpful — a real credit to her parents. I was most impressed, I judged Tony to be in his forties, a good-looking guy about 5'10" with a slim build. I liked Tony right from the word go.

I asked the both of them whether it was alright if I just took a look around. I was impressed by the shop — the layout was great. There were racks all along the back wall, all full of lots of albums. There were also two other racks in the

The Swinging Sixties

middle of the shop, each containing albums, but not too many. Tony, I perceived, was a man of vision, wanting room for more stock as it became available. After looking through the stock I went back to where Tony and Lucy were. I asked them if they still had any new copies of The Beatles' debut album, *Please Please Me*. What an oversight, how could I have forgotten that it was released on the 22nd of March and now we were in May. Thankfully they told me that they had two copies. I then asked if it would be possible to get four more copies, to which they replied that it would take at least a couple of days. "Please get them for me," I said, "I will pay upfront." We shook hands and agreed, after which I paid Tony the money, almost completely clearing me out. Luckily, I knew I still had my winnings to come from my bet. We chatted some more, then I left saying, "See you in a couple of days."

I left the shop, walking back the high street, it was now 1:30pm. Feeling rather thirsty because of the warm sun, I looked for a sweet shop where I could get a drink with the change I had left over. Just as I found a shop, two teenage boys appeared out of the door, each with a large bottle of coke. They began shaking them and spraying each other. I ended up caught in the middle of the spray, leading the two boys to say in concert, "Sorry, mister." *At least they are having fun*, I thought. I went into the shop and got myself a drink.

Mint Vinyl

I was now back on Thomas Street, walking back towards the bookies. Just as I was walking past Ivy Road, I heard the voice of a woman, shouting loudly. At first, I didn't see her, then running towards me, I realised she was in great distress — tears streaming down her face. She was shouting over and over, "Please help. Fire! My baby is upstairs!" Looking back from where she had run, I saw smoke billowing from a terraced house. I grabbed her by the arms asking her how old her baby was. "Eighteen months old, a little girl — Avril," she replied. Without thinking I ran into the house. The smoke was already quite thick, *I have to be quick*, I thought. I reached into my trouser pocket for my handkerchief. I tied it around my nose and my mouth and ran upstairs. The fire seemed small but there was a large amount of smoke. I found a bedroom and going in I found a cot at the bedside. There was the baby crying loudly in obvious distress. I picked her up and made my way downstairs. Gasping for breath, I made it out into the street. Looking at the child, it seemed that she had not been hurt. As I continued down the street, the baby's mother ran towards me, holding out her arms. I gave the child to her, tears still flowing down her cheeks — now tears of joy. She thanked me over and over again. I was simply glad to have been able to help. By this time a large crowd was gathering, and I could hear a fire engine approaching. I felt a sudden need to get away from the scene; awkward questions were

The Swinging Sixties

the last thing I wanted. I very quickly slipped away down the street, making my way back onto Thomas Street.

After walking for a while, not really noticing where I had been walking, it seemed that I had wandered off the main street and walked down several others. I stopped on a street corner, having no real idea where I was. I looked around for a street sign, finding one which read 'Elliot Street'. I could clearly see a small park down near the end of the street. Children were happily playing with their parents watching on. I made my way over to some benches that I could see. I sat down with my head spinning. I needed to rest and come to my senses. After what seemed like hours (in reality only about twenty minutes or so) I began to be able to think a little clearer. My initial thoughts were to get back home, but then, reflecting on what had just happened, I realised that I needed to formulate some kind of plan. I made a real conscious effort to gather my thoughts and think this thing through. The question came to mind, *Should I go to the bookies and get my winnings?* The answer was a resounding yes. Because I had rushed into that house and rescued the baby Avril without thinking of the consequences, I needed to finish what I was doing. I had no intentions of returning to this situation because, even if I just came back in time for the bookies, I couldn't know if Avril would still be safe if I was not there—I could not know the answer. What had at first seemed like such an easy thing—travelling back in time—now seemed so very complicated.

Mint Vinyl

I was now at least thinking more clearly, and at this point needed to find some public toilets, as I was looking a mess with all that smoke. After a bit of searching, and having to ask someone, I was directed to some toilets. Thankfully they were large ones, with a good number of sinks, and some mirrors. Going in, I quickly found that my suspicions had been correct. The smoke had blackened my face, hair, and hands, as well as my shirt, jacket, and trousers. I cleaned myself up to the best of my ability, with the help of paper towels. After washing my hands and face, I was at least feeling better. Returning to the park bench, I spent some time just sitting in the sun, drying out my clothes, after my attempts to clean them up.

After a while I made my way back towards the bookies, asking once again for directions. Here I was back at Clifton Road. Going in, I gave Mark Stanley my betting slip. He looked closely at it, checked his book, and said, "Your lucky day today, pal, two winners." Just then, the man himself emerged from the back.

"Two winners," he said. Giving me some sort of snarl, he went back into the rear of the shop muttering obscenities to himself—he was not a happy bunny our Dave. I collected my winnings and left. At least no one had mentioned my appearance, which cheered me up a little. I now made my way back to the canal towpath to my apartment building—well at least to where it would be.

The Swinging Sixties

Within a couple of minutes, I was safely back in my lounge. I must have just collapsed onto my sofa, thinking of the day's events over and over in my mind. I took off my clothes and put them into the wash, then took a shower. After this, I made a ready meal I'd bought, thinking while I ate it, *remind me not to buy any more of these*. It was gross! Making myself a sandwich instead and a brew, I began to properly think through the day's events. I didn't for one minute regret saving young Avril's life, but it had nonetheless brought into sharp focus the need to be much more careful in the future, or was that the past? I thought of the very beginning of my adventures, of how thrilled and excited I was to be going into the past. But now I began to realise that the past could be fraught with dangers. I concluded that I must, to the best of my ability, try to keep out of situations where people would want to know more about me. However, the day was not a complete disaster, I had some more money now, and best of all I had met Tony and his daughter Lucy (and I was about to meet Tony's wife Janette). On the 3rd of May 1963, I was scheduled to go back to Hibbert's record shop to pick up my Beatles albums. I was now able to buy some others as well, courtesy of Mr Rossi. I was due in work in the morning, so I planned to visit Tony after work.

The next day passed okay, nothing much to say, except maybe as someone once said it was much ado about nothing. Having returned home from work, I made preparations for my trip to Tony's place — my thoughts were filled with it. During the day I had thought that it would be a really great idea if I could become a good friend to Tony and his family. I had also been thinking that just like my efforts in the present to be normal were going much better, I also needed to be as normal as possible in the past. I needed to look after myself, making sure to eat and drink, because for me it was so easy to forget. I didn't know it yet, but events were going to go a long way in seeing that these very things would be done.

I once more returned to 1963, arriving at Tony's shop. Going in, I once again received a warm welcome. Tony told me right away that he had got my albums, and that he had also done what I had requested. I had asked Tony to give me a separate receipt for each album I would purchase. I thought that this would be a good touch for the resale of the records — customer satisfaction. I then began pulling out a few more albums that I wanted, Tony cashed it all up, and I settled my bill. Just at this time there was a lull in trade, as normally the shop would be full. This gave me a chance to speak more with Tony. He was a really admirable guy, and I could tell that he was really smart too. We talked about records and things in general. I then happened to mention that I had called into Dave Rossi's betting shop, to which Tony said, "Was he there?"

"He came in as I was leaving," I replied. "He seems a happy soul, doesn't he?"

The Swinging Sixties

Tony Immediately got my drift and gave a big smile saying, "That's Dave alright." Tony continued, "Apart from that, what do you think of Dave?"

I replied, "He looks like a bit of a thug to me."

Tony laughed and responded, "Yes, he certainly is." Tony then went on to tell me about Dave's three cronies, known locally as Rossi's posse. The first was Kevin Wilson, second in command—six feet tall, very stocky and muscular, chiselled features, and some might say craggy—not what you might call an oil painting, but he was his mother's son! Next was Len Pearce. Len was in his late thirties, just a bit younger than Wilson. This guy was just absolutely full of tattoos with a face like a battered clog, missing teeth, you name it that was Len. Last was Brian Thorpe, also a big guy. Each of the three looked every inch a nasty piece of work. You wouldn't want to meet them on a dark night.

Tony said, "Listen, Jack, it will be lunchtime soon, so how do you fancy going down to the local chippy? They have a sit in place there, what do you think, mate?"

"Sounds great," I said, "whenever you're ready." So off we went to the local chippy on Robinson Road about ten minutes away from Tony's shop. We ate our meal of fish, chips, and peas, which by the way was delicious. I then said to Tony, "So, tell me a little more about yourself." Tony told me that about his wife Janette and their daughter Lucy. He also told me that he'd always had a passion for music and had taken over his dad's business when he died; his mum

Mint Vinyl

having no interest in it. He also had a very keen interest in electronics. I was amazed at how much we had in common. We talked some more, then Tony told me that he would have to get back to the shop, as he couldn't leave Lucy on her own for too long.

Before he went Tony said, "One last thing, Jack, well two actually. You said that you were new to the area, well where do you live?" This question caught me off guard, I had to think on my feet. *What should I say? I can't tell him my real address*, I thought. Luckily, I remembered that when I had first arrived in the 1960s, I had seen that phase one of the Firsgrove Estate had been built. Feeling sure that Tony would know this I told him that that's where I lived. He in turn just said, "Okay." *Phew that was close*, I thought to myself. Then Tony said, "There were two things, the other is that I'd like us to be good friends, I really like you, Jack. What do you think about coming for your tea on Monday night?"

I at once said, "That would be fantastic."

"See you then, about 6pm."

Tony then left, I sat in the chippy for a while longer then left, the bill having already been paid by Tony. I made my way back home, my real house I mean. On returning I was so pleased with how things had gone. I had some friends in the sixties, *How great was that?* I thought. Little did I know what lay ahead for me, Tony, and his family. Looking back on my trip into the sixties I thought, *People call them the*

The Swinging Sixties

swinging sixties? Where I had been in the town of Dansford I didn't think it was. Sure, everywhere seemed much brighter and more colourful that the fifties... but swinging... no. Knowing that I could go see Tony anytime I wanted was a great comfort to me. I passed the rest of the week going to work and began making more preparations for what I now believed would lead to the fulfilment of all my dreams.

Chapter 6

Tony's Workshop

I awoke on Saturday morning feeling refreshed. It was a lovely day outside. I put some coffee on and made some toast, and then decided to spend some time sitting out on my balcony. I spent an hour or so out there. I then went to my wardrobe to pick out some clothes for my visit to Tony's. I wanted to look smart but not too overdressed. Now being ready, I went into the lounge and turned on the radio. Getting my notepad, I jotted down all the relevant information. I had decided that after my trip I was going to start using my mobile phone, as well as my notepad, to store all the data that I needed for my future trips into the past. I had also decided to keep a record of exactly where, as well as when, I had gone during my trips—not wanting to risk inadvertently running into myself in future—or should I say, in the past. I wasn't sure if this could happen, but I was in unfamiliar territory. I was feeling ready, albeit with some trepidation—this was a big thing, and I was hoping that very good things would come out of meeting Tony and his family in a relaxed atmosphere. I was also looking forward

Mint Vinyl

to meeting Tony's wife Janette, who Tony had described as a great cook, and a wonderful wife and mother. Tony also said that she didn't often help out in the shop because she had her own job. She was the manager of a local laundry — a busy woman. I set all the displays and was ready for my next encounter with the sixties.

Having arrived, I made my way to Tony's shop, which had just closed — or should I say almost, as the last customers were just making their way out as I arrived. At the door, Tony gave me a big smile saying, "Jack, so good to see you again." We walked in and Tony lifted up the counter saying, "Come in, Jack, welcome to our place." Tony went ahead through the door, switching on a light — when I say light, it was in fact a number of lights. It was a large room with benches on two of the walls, cabinets here and there, a very large bench in the middle of the room, and stools pushed up to the benches. On the benches were parts of TVs and radios — they were everywhere. There were also a good number of record players of all shapes and sizes. Here and there on the benches were individual swivel lights with magnifying glasses, and soldering irons. It was incredible, a veritable Aladdin's cave.

"Well, what do you think of my workshop, Jack?" Tony asked.

I didn't really know what to say at first, I was gobsmacked but wasn't sure if that was an appropriate thing to say in this era, so I just said, "It's brilliant, Tony."

Tony's Workshop

"Yeah, it is," Tony replied, "just wish I had more time to spend in here." Most of the stuff was Tony's, but he did repair things for friends as well. We then walked through another door, which led into a very cosy dining room, where Janette and Lucy were busy laying the table. It was a bright room, tastefully decorated, with few pieces of furniture apart from the large dining table and six chairs. There were some pictures on the walls — landscapes, Constable if I was not mistaken.

"Very impressive," I said to Tony. Leading from the dining room was the kitchen, another large room very nicely set out with good equipment of the day. Tony's wife and daughter made several trips from the kitchen to the dining room.

"Is everything ready now, dear?" asked Tony. Having received a nod from his wife, Tony said, "I'm sorry, Jack, I should have taken your jacket." Doing so he disappeared into a cupboard, returning very quickly. "Right, take a seat, everyone."

Janette and Lucy had prepared a lovely meal. Lots of veg, roast and mashed potatoes, roast beef, and Yorkshire puddings, with apple pie and custard for afters. Tony was right, his missus was a really good cook — I was absolutely stuffed. After the meal, Tony and I went into the lounge. The room was very large indeed. Most of the walls were cream coloured, but along the wall with the fireplace was a lovely shade of red. There was no fire lit at the time, but it was a

Mint Vinyl

beautiful ornate fireplace — black and gold. There were two large leather sofas and two large chairs, as well as a particularly lovely piece of furniture which I had guessed from my research was a radiogram. My assumption proved to be correct once everyone was in the room and Tony turned on the radio — at a low level but still producing a rather nice tone. There had of course been some introductions over dinner, and of course some conversations, but now I hoped there would be an opportunity to really get to know Tony and his lovely wife and daughter. I asked Tony and his family lots of things, not only in an effort to get to know them more, but also to keep the conversation away from myself as much as possible. I told them that I was into electronics and that I had a lifelong passion for music. Tony was very much taken by just how alike we were, as I had been when first talking to Tony.

I asked Tony, "How long have you been here for?"

"Ten years now," he replied, "it was my dad's shop, but when he died, we took over. Dad did okay, but I like to think that things are better now. Just a minute, I will show you what I mean." Tony then left the room for a few minutes.

I took the opportunity to talk to Janette, asking her about her job. She said that she had started as a laundry assistant and worked her way up to where she was now. While Lucy was busy enjoying the songs on the radio, Tony returned with a photo album, a sort of before and after thing. They had clearly put a lot of work into the shop, Tony having pre-

Tony's Workshop

viously worked for a small TV and radio repair business. But now, the shop was his life, and though not directly on the high street, Tony's shop was a thriving one. This was down mostly to Tony and Lucy's hard work, both being very knowledgeable about the record business, and Tony having some very good contacts. All in all, I thought the night had gone extremely well so far.

The topic of conversation inevitably turned to me. I tried to keep what I divulged to a minimum, without seeming too evasive. After a night cap it was time for me to leave. Saying my goodbyes, Tony showed me to the door. I thanked him once again for a brilliant evening, asking him if we could meet up again, as I had a proposition to put to him.

"That would be great," he said, "I'm busy all next week, but how's about next Friday night at the shop?"

"That's great," I said, "I'll be popping into the shop now and then before Friday."

Tony replied, "Okay, see you when I see you."

It was getting dark as I made my way to the canal towpath. Seeing just a couple of courting couples on the way there, I smiled to myself as I walked, thinking, *How good was that?* This had been by far my best trip into the past.

I reached home at the same time as I had left. That was the beauty of Uncle George's machine. I began to think of the wonderful legacy that Uncle George had left for me, never realising that things could change—but, for the present, I was happy. I made myself a rum and coke, going back

Mint Vinyl

onto my balcony to enjoy the very lovely day. After spending a couple of hours out there, I came back inside to get my phone, in order to put in my information. That done, I sat down on the sofa, thinking about my next meeting with Tony. My idea was to obtain from him most of the records that I would need. My ultimate goal was to have my own shop — but that's in the future. I didn't really know when that might happen. I knew that I must try to remember to visit Tony's shop at the right times, not making the same mistake as before. That was the reason behind the phone — so I could have all of the relevant information with me. If I could reach some agreement with Tony then it would be very good for not only me, but also for Tony's business. I did not anticipate too many obstacles to my plan.

As things had been a little slow at work, I decided that I would take a holiday — a whole week off work. I would then be able to take the opportunity to do more research and find more things for my ever-expanding wardrobe. One thing that I really needed was some sort of carry case for the records that I would buy. Later on, I contacted work to sort out my holiday. With that now sorted, I got changed and drove into town. I bought the ideal case that I needed, as well as some essentials for home.

After I got back home, I spent the rest of Saturday just chilling out and listening to some of my music. Later that evening I phoned my mum. She had moved into number 14 Sycamore Lane — Uncle George's old house had been left to

Tony's Workshop

her in his will. Having now sorted out her affairs, she had left the property that she had rented with my dad. Mum had been on her own for many years since Dad passed away as a result of never really recovering from his accident, dying of a heart attack. Anyway, that being said, I had told my mum I would pay her a visit now that she was at number 14.

After a good night's sleep, and a good breakfast, I decided to walk to Mum's — with it being another nice day. I really enjoy the walk there. Seeing a number of people that I knew, I exchanged pleasantries, as you do. I must say that I felt full of the joys of spring that morning. I could hardly believe it, two lovely days in a row, *Must be some kind of record*, I thought. I spent a few hours with Mum reminiscing mostly about Uncle George and Auntie Suzanne. Mum had been invited on many occasions to move in with Uncle George and Auntie Suzanne, but for some reason known only to herself, she had always said no. I didn't feel the need to press for an answer. Saying goodbye to Mum, I set off back home.

It was still nice and bright on my homeward journey. As I walked back, I bumped into Uncle George's old friend Joe Foster with his dog Patch. We said hello, then, out of the blue, Joe said, "How's the record collection going on?"

"Very well actually, Joe," I said. "Thanks for asking."

Mint Vinyl

We said goodbye then walked our separate ways. As I walked home, I couldn't help thinking to myself that the record collecting was going to get a whole lot better.

Making it back home, I went straight to the kitchen and prepared myself a nice salad with boiled potatoes and eggs. I had only had a gallon of tea and some biscuits at Mum's place. *Afterwards I'll just relax for a while*, I thought. Putting on a record, I started to relax on the sofa. Next thing I knew, the record had finished, and I had woken up with a stiff neck. I began to think of visiting Tony, hoping that we would be able to reach an agreement about the albums I needed. I made a list in my note pad, as I couldn't do it on my phone—I very well couldn't show that to Tony. I sure did want to strengthen my friendship with him, but in some ways, it was like walking on eggshells, not wanting to say the wrong thing. I tried to watch some TV, but it was no use. Just a load of old tripe on again. To an observer my life must have seemed a lonely one, and in some ways it was. But as a private kind of person, I didn't have many friends, not really good friends anyway. I could have counted them on two fingers: one had emigrated to New Zealand; the other was married with two young kids. So, my friendship with Tony was really important to me, being on the same level in lots of ways (although he was happily married). Anyway, enough of the self-pity. I got a tot of rum and headed off to bed. *No need for an alarm for tomorrow, whoopee,* I thought.

Tony's Workshop

I awoke to a new day, with my clock saying 8:15pm, and drew the blinds. I knew it was too good to be true — very dull and drizzling. There couldn't be three nice days — just too much to ask I guess. I chose some clothes from my wardrobe: a pair of jeans, nice shirt, lightweight jacket, and a pair of brown shoes — not very trendy, but at least they matched my jacket. I didn't know what the weather was like in sixty-three yet, but I would soon find out.

Making sure that I had everything with me, I went into the lounge, switched on the radio, got the specs, set the displays, and pressed the centre white button, and, hey presto, away I went. The fracture became stable, and I saw that in '63 it was not too bad of a day, a bit dull… but fine. I walked forward and down the towpath — a place now very familiar to me. I walked in the direction of Tony's shop, but I must have been a little later this time, as the shop was already closed. I knocked on the door, a light went on, and Lucy opened the door. She gave me a lovely smile and a hug, saying, "Come on in, Jack. Dad is expecting you." We walked through the workshop, which seemed even more stuffed with lots of electrical goods. We then reached the dining room table where Tony was.

He reached out to grab my hand saying, "Good to see you, Jack my friend."

"Likewise, Tony."

"Take a seat, Jack. So, you say that you have a proposition for me?"

Mint Vinyl

"Yes, yes I have, Tony."

"Put the kettle on, Lucy, please, my love. Make us a nice strong brew, you know how I like it." As Lucy went into the kitchen, Tony spoke again, "Janet is out at a friend's tonight, a woman from work. So, it will be just me and thee so to speak. Lucy will go listening to music when she's brewed up." We got our drinks then got down to business. "So, what can I do for you, Jack?"

I replied, "I would like you to supply me with any albums, or singles for that matter, that I may require. I will need a quite a few copies of each item. It will be good for me and make some good money for you. I am a collector as you know, Tony, but I also sell records as well. I want to assure you that my selling records won't affect your business — not one little bit. I know you will have questions about all this, like where I will be selling them, but on some of it I will just have to ask you to trust me. Please, Tony, just trust me. It's not anything dodgy. I'm not Dave Rossi, and while we're on the subject, I don't think he's very pleased with me. I've been in the shop a few times and picked some winners. He was there when I picked up my winnings, and said to me, 'the only person who should be winning in my shop is the guy on my side of the counter,' adding that he thought that there was something different about me, how I was always winning, and that he would get to the bottom of it." Albeit that this was absolutely true, this was said as a kind of smoke screen for Tony. But he was having none of it.

Tony replied, "Well, Jack, two things. Firstly, I know we haven't known each other for years or anything, but I already feel a bond between us. We are so alike in many ways, so I do, and I will trust you, Jack. About the records, it does seem a little strange, but that's okay. But number two you definitely should be worried about. You don't want to go upsetting Rossi and his posse, Jack. He's a nasty piece of work, well known for sorting people out who ruffle his feathers, if you follow my drift. You've got to watch yourself with them, Jack. He's not just going to let it go."

"I appreciate that, Tony, but I meant no harm. I just like to have a flutter on the gee gees, that's all. Now, getting back to my proposal, I will require a good number of albums and singles, and, as a show of my appreciation for trusting me, how's about this: I'll help you out in your workshop with your projects and your repairs."

He gave me a big smile and said, "Listen, it's a deal."

I was so pleased that Tony was flowing with my plans. *Working with him will be just great*, I thought, *it will strengthen our friendship even more, I can't wait*. I said goodnight to Tony and shouted to Lucy in the other room saying goodnight.

I had an uneventful journey home. Once back, I began to write down some of my plans. I needed to expand my business, make changes to my website, and contact my personal clients by phone. I wanted to move a few steps closer to ful-

Mint Vinyl

filling my ambition concerning 'Mint Vinyl'. I had long held the idea that I would always sell my records at, what you would call, very reasonable prices. Yet, I wanted to make myself some money. I also loved the idea of just blowing people's minds when they got a mint copy of their favourite band or whatever. So, I decided to spend some time on my website, and I planned to call my clients the next day. For now, I felt a warm glow. *I have some good friends,* I thought — even if they were in a different era. My plans, hopes, and dreams seemed to be being realised. *I am, for once, very happy with my lot,* I thought. Later on, I made a meal for myself, and then, as I would not be at work in the morning, I put on some music and had a nice tot of rum before going to bed. *It's been a good day,* I thought to myself.

    The next morning came around, and I made my usual preparations. I do like my routine; it brings me comfort. I know I'm a saddo, but there you go, that's just me. Anyways, radio on, specs too, the displays set, off I went. Well, it was another nice day. *That's what I like to see,* I thought. The sun was shining, and all was well with the world — apart from the fact that there will be a little trouble for the government about some call girls, but that's another story. Arriving at Tony's place, I went in and received my usual greetings. I had brought my carry case with me, as well the list of the things I needed. I walked over to speak to Tony and Lucy, giving him the list of items from my pocket.

Tony's Workshop

"Some of them are not out till sometime later this month," I said.

Tony looked at the list, and then at me, and said, "How do you know these things? Don't tell me, it's a secret."

I then asked Tony, "Sometimes I may need some imported stuff, would that be possible?"

"Probably," he answered, "I'll ask my contacts, but it will probably take a while to get them."

"No probs," I said. Tony just glanced at me. I realised that I say a few things which may seem a bit strange to Tony and Lucy. I had a good look in the racks, finding a couple of albums I wanted for myself. Buying these, I said to Tony, "See you about six, so we can do some stuff in the workshop."

"Okay, Jack,' he replied, "see you then."

"Yes, see you, Uncle Jack," shouted Lucy. I was well pleased with that.

Before I went back home, I paid a visit to my friendly bookmakers. I went in and immediately Dave was glaring at me. *If looks could kill eh*, I thought, *I would surely be dead*. The first words out of his mouth were, "Not you in here again. I don't like you... I don't like anything about you."

"That's not very nice, Dave," I said, "I'm a paying customer."

He snapped back, "Yeah, and you always take out more than you ever put in, and I definitely don't like that."

"Well, can I put my bets on or what?"

73

Mint Vinyl

"I'm thinking of barring you."

Without thinking I answered, "Whatever," in a very cynical way.

"See, there you go again, who says things like that? I've told you, there's something funny about you, and don't mean ha ha. I'm telling you, Jack, or whatever your name is, if you win again, you're barred for life."

I took my slip and left the shop. I had a bit of time to kill for the races, so I wandered around for a while, mainly looking for another bookies. Thankfully, in this town, it was not too difficult—I found several, making notes of them in my pad. Then, I went into the local café for something to eat. While I was in there waiting for the races to end, I began to reflect on what Tony had said about Dave Rossi. *But he's just so easy to wind up*, I thought, *it's like there's a big key in his back—I just can't help myself—and besides that, I need the money.*

The time came for me to go back to Dave's. I knew what was going to happen, because I would win my bets again, then Dave would bar me. When I walked in, I almost broke out into laughter and Dave's face was an absolute picture. He snarled, "I told you what would happen if you won again. Here, take your winnings and get out of my shop. Shut the door and don't come back!"

As I was on the way out, I heard him telling his two shop workers to never let me bet again. I wasn't really looking forward to telling Tony that evening when I went to help

Tony's Workshop

him out in the workshop. I decided that I would make my way back home. As I did, I got the distinct feeling that I was being followed. I turned around to see that I was right, it was Kevin Wilson.

He said to me in a very threatening way, "A message from Dave. Don't think that you've heard the last of it. Dave is out for revenge, one way or another."

Arriving back at my apartment, I began to feel very anxious about what had happened. Gone were the smiles, and the somewhat cocky attitude — this was really worrying. After getting in the shower, I just stood there, letting the spray just pulse onto my head and face. My mind was racing. I couldn't get Wilson's face out of my mind. He was a very nasty thug that had crawled out from a rock somewhere. I tried to vainly cheer myself up by thinking disparaging thoughts about him. He was big and tough and very nasty. However, he was far from being bright. In fact, he had the IQ of an ice cube. Afterwards, I just sat and moped for what seemed like hours — in reality it was even less than one hour. *What did he mean?* I thought, *and just how am I going to tell Tony about all this?* I looked at my website and checked the messages on my phone in a vain effort to take my mind off these things. I really was very disturbed about what had taken place — I couldn't contain myself any longer, I would have to go back and tell Tony what I had done.

Chapter 7

Face the Music

I made the journey back to Tony's with my stomach churning and my pulse racing. Tony and Lucy both smiled at me, I smiled back, trying to act normal.

"Won't be long, Jack," said Tony, "just got to see to my last customer of the evening, then I'm yours." After a few more minutes the customer left, and Lucy went through into the house. By this time, I must have been looking a bit pale.

"What's up, Jack?' asked Tony. "You look like you've seen a ghost."

I swallowed, and then thought, *It's time to face the music.* Then, all of a sudden, it just came flooding out like a torrent. So much so, that Tony had to shake me and tell me, "Slow down, Jack. Pull yourself together." At this, I calmed a little and began my tale. "Jack, Jack, what have you done my friend?" said Tony, "You have opened up a very nasty can of worms."

Tony then began to relate to me some of the things both he and Lucy had noticed. He said that it began a while ago. Every time I had come to the shop, one of Rossi's posse had made it his business to be there—all the time watching me very closely. He said that it was the brighter one of the three: Brian Thorpe. *What was Dave up to?* I thought, *sending his man to spy on me?* Tony said that whatever it was, it could only spell trouble for me. I wouldn't have long to wait to find out what it was going to be.

"Will it be okay if I don't stay to help tonight?" I asked Tony. "I'm so sorry, but I just can't concentrate with all of this going on in my head."

"That's alright, Jack," he said, "go home and try to get some rest. We'll sort this out, Jack, don't worry mate." Tony seemed confident about what he had said, but I was still very concerned... and well that I was.

After arriving home, I got dressed to go into town, as I was feeling rather hungry. I found a nice restaurant and had a good meal, after which I felt a little better. I looked around the room and saw this very attractive woman (in her early forties I'd say) looking at me and smiling. She got up and walked over to me.

"On your own?" she said.

I, rather to my shame said sarcastically, "Looks like it, don't you think?"

I apologised to her saying, "Sorry, what's your name?"

"Debra," she replied.

"Well, Debra, once again, sorry for my attitude," I said, "just a really bad day. Maybe I'll see you around."

Face the Music

I got up to leave and pay my bill—she seemed quite stunned. *Well, I thought to myself, I don't need any more complications in my life. Rossi and his posse are quite enough, thank you very much.*

I drove home to my apartment block and, getting back inside, I checked my website and my messages. There had been quite a bit of interest on both. My private connections mostly consisted of people needing stuff that's imported. I made a note of these. Most of the website stuff I already had, so I could easily deal with those. I would have to see Tony about the import stuff.

I decided to go and see Tony that evening. I made all of my preparations and set up the machine. Once more, I was standing on the towpath looking at the now very familiar landscape. Walking towards Tony's shop, my thoughts were occupied not least by the matter of Tony thinking that I must be an idiot for getting in this mess with Rossi—especially when he had warned me not to. Reaching the shop, I was very glad when I still received the regular welcome. There was something very comforting about being in the company of Tony and Lucy (and also Janette whenever she was there). I asked Tony how Janette was doing. "Very well, Jack," said Tony, "but doing a lot of overtime at the moment. Extremely busy at the laundry." Then the conversation inevitably turned to the situation with Rossi. Tony told me that he had had a visit from the local bobby. "It seems a concerned citizen has asked the police to look into this matter concerning you, Jack," he said. My heart sunk. "They, or rather he, Steve Lane, our local bobby, wants you to call in at the station. They contacted me, not having any details about you."

"Okay, I'll have to do that," I said, "I will call in tomorrow."

"I'll go with you if you like, Jack, I would like to support you in this. That Dave Rossi is just a pain. I don't like him at all. One day we must have a serious chat about Dave. I will tell you things that will make your hair curl."

Then I said to Tony, "I have come to give you a hand in the workshop."

"That's great, Jack," he replied, "I'm getting somewhat behind with my repairs, the help would be seriously appreciated." Not boasting, but this kind of work was nothing to me, pretty simple technology really. To Tony's joy we completed all of his outstanding repairs. Having been thanked over and over again by Tony for my help, I said, "See you tomorrow. What time will be okay for you?"

"10:30am."

"Alright, that's fine, see you then." We shook hands and I left. It was beginning to stay lighter now that the months were going on. It was a fine night, and I had a pleasant walk back to the towpath. I touched my specs and set the display. I arrived back in my lounge and, after sitting for a few moments, my mind began to focus on what to do the next day. *The police will probably want some form of identification,* I thought, *that could be a problem in 1963, as I don't have an identification card, and I can't magic one up from somewhere. Something else will have to suffice.* After many hours of research, I had decided to do certain things: open up a bank account; join the library (so I would have a card); and a local social club (so I would have a membership card) — all, unfortunately, containing a false address. I had looked around Firsgrove Estate and noted an address of an unoccupied house which still had its curtains, so, for all intents and purposes, I could use it as part of my cover. The address was number 23 Ethel Street on the Firsgrove Estate, Dansford. I can't say that I was filled with confidence in these things, but I was doing my best.

Making myself a snack and a brew, I listened to the radio for a while. Then, beginning to tire, I headed off to my bed. I slept quite well, waking up around 6:30am to the birds singing — no, not my neighbours, the feathered variety. Feeling hungry, I prepared a full English, mopping up my plate with a slice of bread, and polishing off a good strong brew. Not wanting to give the wrong impression, I decided on a shirt and tie, black trousers, and a smart leather jacket. After checking I had everything I needed with me, I went through the preparations, and off I went to go and meet Tony.

I reached the shop at 10:25am, with Tony already outside. We shook hands and headed off to the cop shop. We entered, with me feeling a little bit nervous I must admit. Tony grabbed me by the shoulder saying, "Come on, mate, let's

Mint Vinyl

do it." Walking up to the front desk we talked to Sergeant Billy Lamb. Tony knew him and greeted him.

"This way," Sergeant Lamb said. He then shouted to PC Lane to take over the desk, "Won't be long, lad, hold the fort."

Sergeant Lamb then led me into a small room containing only two chairs and a desk, and the Sergeant and I took a seat.

The Sergeant began, "Now, Mr Roberts..."

"Jack," I interjected.

"I know," he replied, "but I have to keep this formal." He continued, "Well, Mr Roberts, a member of the public has made some accusations concerning you. That's why you're here this morning."

"What are they, Sergeant?" I asked.

"That you have won on horse racing bets an unusual number of times. Twelve times I'm told."

"So, it's Rossi who complained, sir?"

"I have a duty to perform, now if you don't mind, can you shed any light on these things?"

"All I can say is, that as far as Mr Rossi's betting shop is concerned, I must be very lucky indeed. If you check at several other betting shops in town, you'll find that I don't always win."

"We'll look into that, sir. Now, there is also another matter concerning Mr Hibbert's record shop. You have been purchasing a large quantity of records have you not?"

Face the Music

"I have, sergeant, but all with my friend Tony's permission."

"Why so many of the same records then?"

"The truth is, sergeant, I am a record agent who purchases records for private collectors who wish to remain, as it were, anonymous. I'm sure you can appreciate someone wanting their privacy, Sergeant Lamb."

"Quite well, sir, quite. Well, I think that's all gentlemen, we will be in touch. One last thing, do you have any form of identification, Mr Roberts? Just a formality, you understand."

"I seem to have misplaced my ID card, but I do have these." I showed him my bank book, library card, and membership card for the Dansford social club. He looked at them and handed them back.

"Do you have your address, sir?"

"23 Ethel Street," I told him, even though it was on the things I showed him. *Seems that the police are the police whenever you see them*, I thought.

Sergeant Lamb said once again, "We'll be in touch when we complete our inquiries. Thank you, Mr Roberts, that will be all for now." In the next breath he bellowed to PC Lane, "Come on, lad, quick about it, get to those bookies in town!"

About two weeks later, we got a visit from Sergeant Billy Lamb himself, calling in at Tony's place when I happened to be there helping Tony in his workshop. He told us that they had completed their inquiries and that they required no further action. At this time, he bid us a good evening and left. "That's good news eh, Jack," said Tony.

"It certainly is, Tony," I replied — although I'd like to bet, if you'll pardon the pun, that a certain Mr Dave Rossi wasn't so happy. Anyway, for now I tried to forget all about Rossi and his posse; although it was hard to do as Brian Thorpe still kept up his presence at the shop. He wasn't the sharpest tool in the shed, but compared to Kevin Wilson, he was an Albert Einstein.

In the coming weeks my friendship with Tony grew and grew. We spent many hours together in his workshop, and I was invited on a few occasions for tea, where I got much better acquainted with Janette and Lucy — what a great family! I hadn't felt so much love between people since Uncle George and my Auntie Suzanne. One night, while working with Tony in his workshop, he asked me, "Are you doing anything on Friday night?"

I replied, "No, why? You don't normally work Friday; you always say it's your one night off."

"That's right," said Tony, "how do you fancy coming to the local pub Friday night?"

The day being Thursday I replied, "That would be great."

"Are you good at darts?"

"Not bad at all actually, if I say so myself."

"One of our team can't make it tomorrow, so you are it, Jack."

"Where is it, Tony?"

"We're at home this week, 'The Falconers' on the corner of Ryle Street, off the main road just after the traffic lights. Do you know where I mean? Or do you want to meet at the shop?"

"No, I'll meet you at the pub."

"Great, looking forward to it." And so was I, my life at that moment was going really well. Even Brian Thorpe had stopped coming into the shop. Things were just brilliant; I can't put into words how good I felt.

The next day I was in my apartment getting ready to go to 'The Falconers'. I got dressed, putting on a smart blue shirt, no tie this time, but my leather jacket though, and some denims. I stood in front of the mirror thinking to myself, *Yeah, I'm looking pretty cool*. I turned on the radio, and with the dial showing red, I put on my specs. With great excitement I set my displays and soon I was on the towpath.

It was 6:30pm on Friday night. It was a lovely balmy evening with lots of people about. I made my way to the pub, it being almost 7pm when I got there. I went in and the smoke and the noise suddenly hit me. *Wow this is different*, I thought, not having been in a pub in the sixties before, I'd forgotten people could still smoke — and the air was thick with it. I saw Tony at the bar, standing with this guy. He was about 5' 6", bald head, little moustache, and quite a raspberry going on. "Bert, this is Jack I was telling you about," Tony said.

"Hi, Jack," said Bert, "nice to meet you."

Mint Vinyl

"Likewise," I said. It was then, whilst I was close up to him, his chin, or should I say chins, he looked just like he was looking over the top of half a dozen muffins. I smiled to myself thinking, *Tony knows some characters.*

"How's it going, Jack?" asked Bert, "Tony tells me you've been working with him." I couldn't help but notice that Bert had a Welsh accent when he said, "From the Valleys originally isn't it. People call me Bertie or Boyo — well, that's my darts name."

As we were getting acquainted, another guy walked up. Tony smiled and shook his hand firmly. This guy was easily 6', and very muscular and, as Tony told me, into weightlifting — hence his darts name: Paul 'the body' Carter. Tony was known as Tony 'LP' Hibbert for obvious reasons, and there was me: Jack 'Robbo' Roberts — what a team!

As the match progressed, we were not doing as well as I had hoped. We were playing a team from Sansfield, a town about ten miles from Dansford — good they were too. It was Bertie's turn at the hockey, when Paul Carter slapped him on the back saying, "Come on, Bertie, you can do it. We've got the arrows."

To which Bertie turned and said, "So did the Apaches, and look what happened to them." You've got to laugh — a great bunch of guys. The beer flowed all night, we also had potato pie with a crust — it was really tasty. We had a fantastic night, even if we did lose the match. We said our goodbyes, and Tony and I staggered back to the shop, singing as we went along.

When we reached the shop I said, "Thanks for a great night, pal, thanks for asking me."

"See you tomorrow then."

"Sleep well, my mate." After this we both started to laugh. I made my way back to the tow path a little slower than normal, not always in a straight line, but feeling on top of the world

Chapter 8

A Trip Out

I had even begun to feel much more contented at work. If I were to stretch a point, I might even say that I was perky. My business was growing and, with more and more orders coming in, I was starting to make some good money. However, there was a way to go before I could realise my goal: the 'Mint Vinyl' record shop. Things were still brilliant with Tony and his family — I made regular trips to the shop, both to buy records, and to work with Tony in the evening. I had been mostly relegated to being a spectator at the darts matches — Wee Wille Johnson being back in the fold. I was cutting down on my liquid intake as well.

One summer evening, Tony said, "How do you fancy a trip out, Jack?" I had already been out with Tony in his car on a number of occasions, visiting some of Tony's contacts in the record business and picking up imported albums. Tony had really come up trumps for me so many times. Things were quiet on the Rossi front, and I had been keeping well away from his shop. Anyway, back to Tony's question. "A trip to where?" I asked.

Mint Vinyl

"Blackpool," he said, "it's all arranged. You just need to say yes. A good friend is going to look after the shop, so if it's a yes, you, me, Janette, and Lucy will be off to Blackpool for three days. Well, what do you say, Jack?"

"I'd be delighted," I said.

"The weather should be good according to the weatherman, but we'll see on that one. Planning to go Saturday–Sunday–Monday. Going to set off about 9 o'clock Saturday morning, Jack, come to the shop."

When I got back home, the first thing I did was check the wardrobe. *I think I'll have to hit the charity shops for some new gear*, I thought. I booked the Monday off from work and packed my bags in great anticipation for our trip. I went to the shop on Saturday morning to find Tony packing up the boot of the car. The car was a Vauxhall Cresta — nice motor, four door saloon, two shades of blue. Janette and Lucy came out to the car while Tony was giving some last instructions for his mate about the shop. Tony got in the car, and we were off on our way to Blackpool. I was sat in the front with Tony, so I had a glance at the fuel gauge. *That's good, it's full*, I thought to myself, *there won't be any need to make stops, unless someone needs the loo*. I asked Tony which way he was going to go. He looked at me a bit strangely and said, "The usual way of course." It seemed so funny not driving there on the motorway. Everyone was in high spirits, with Tony and I just talking about this and that, and Janette and Lucy giggling every now and then, obviously about girly things.

A Trip Out

Tony eventually turned on the radio, and everyone started to sing along. The sun was shining, and we were on our way to Blackpool — it seemed like all was well with the world.

The roads were not too busy, and Tony was a good driver. It seemed that in no time at all, we were approaching Blackpool, and I could see the tower. It had been a long time since I had visited the resort. We arrived at Albert Street, the 'Hotel Marlborough'. Going in, we were greeted by the proprietor, Betty Collins, and her husband Joe. Betty was a striking woman in her early 50s — five feet, seven inches tall I would say, slim build, and a large beehive hairdo — still a good-looking lady. Her husband, on the other hand, looked quite a bit older. I was to learn later that he was only two years older — her senior must have had a hard life. Joe was about five foot two, bald, and stocky, with a thin pencilled-in moustache. I only knew that he was bald because of a photo on the wall in the dining room — every time I saw him, he was wearing a chef's hat. Mrs C ran the hotel in military fashion — her word was law — while Joe did all the cooking. I must say that this unlikely couple made a great team. The hotel was spotless, and the meals generous — very delicious.

We had arrived 10:15am, but breakfast had ended at 9:30am on the dot. So, after being shown to our rooms by the maid, we decided to have our breakfast in town. It already had the makings of a lovely day. After having breakfast in a local café, for which I insisted on paying for, telling Tony that it was my treat for having been invited to come along, we returned to the hotel, sorted out our bags, met in the hallway, and decided to take a stroll down the promenade. We were walking along the golden mile, smelling the hot dogs, burgers, and fried onions, and listening to the shouts of the bingo callers inviting the crowds to play. There were already lots of people on the mile. It brought back memories for me of the times I had visited the resort. It was just the sights and sounds of summer. We saw the shops selling buckets and spades, and bats and balls. We bought a ball for the beach, and, after a while, got some deck chairs and went onto the beach. The vendor gave us a demonstration of how to put them up, but Tony and I did not give him much attention — *How hard can it be?* I thought. Well, after a few hilarious attempts, Janette and Lucy took over putting them up while we stood by scratching our heads. We had a great time playing with the ball. It was just so good to be with Tony and his family. I was so relaxed — it felt really good to be there. We had ice cream, we talked, and just sat in our chairs enjoying the beautiful day.

We had booked full board at the hotel, so we made our way back there after taking back our deck chairs. The meal was of the highest standard. Tony remarked that he would like to stay again sometime. After lunch, we decided on another stroll, this time down to the pleasure beach. By the time we got there we had walked off our lunch and we were ready for some fun. It felt so good to just walk on there, no entrance fee to pay, no wrist band. It looked very different

A Trip Out

to the way I was used to seeing it — although I must confess that it was only on TV ads that I had seen it. We went on lots of the rides, and also many of the stalls, winning some of those useless prizes along the way. I can't begin to express just how good the afternoon had been. The time seemed to fly by.

We had to make our way back, to be in time for our evening meal. Mrs Collins was very strict on mealtimes, and we had no intentions of incurring her wrath. Later that evening, we visited a local pub, 'The Crown & Anchor'. They had some good live music on — it was a really good evening. No one got drunk, but we were all merry, I will say that much. We made our way back to the hotel and settled in for the night.

In the morning, we were all up early and ready for breakfast. We planned a visit to the tower after a walk on the beach. I thought to myself about how much better I felt being there than in my own time. We visited the tower, going to the top. It was another nice day, and we could see for miles up there — a fantastic view. Coming down, we walked along the promenade and went into several of the arcades there. Tony had brought with him a large bag of change. We played the slot machines for hours, sometimes winning but mostly losing, as you do — but it was tremendous fun. We talked and laughed so much that, when it was time for our meal, we all felt exhausted.

Mint Vinyl

After lunch we decided to take a nap. For a while after that, we took a stroll around the many gift shops, buying a few souvenirs. While we were having our evening meal, Tony revealed that he had a surprise for us all that evening. We were all wondering what it might be. After getting changed, Tony said, "Let's go." It was 7:30pm on Sunday the 11th of August 1963. We walked from the hotel with Tony leading the way, the rest of us asking where we were going. All Tony would say was, "You'll see when we get there."

At last, we arrived at the 'ABC Theatre'. When we saw the signs outside, we just couldn't believe our eyes. We were just filled with so much emotion. We were going to see The Beatles—yes, the fab four, how incredible! Tony had gotten tickets from his contacts in the music business. Wow, this was just brilliant, none of us could have ever guessed Tony's surprise. What an evening, absolutely indescribable to be a part of it. It was a night that we would never forget. What a father, husband, and friend Tony really was. We made our way to our hotel just buzzing from the evening. We talked about nothing else on the way back, our minds just swimming with it all. *Just how good was that?* I thought.

We went to breakfast still full of the thoughts of the previous night. It almost seemed unreal by then. It was to be our last day that day, the Monday. Tony had planned that we visit Stanley Park. We went in the car after telling Mrs Collins that we would be out for lunch but back later. We

A Trip Out

spent some time in the park on yet another beautiful day — not a cloud in the sky. We also visited the zoo, seeing the different animals, pulling faces at the monkeys, and each other, laughing and giggling. *Another great day,* I thought.

Later on, we went for fish and chips for lunch. On our way back to the car, Tony and I were walking on ahead. When the car came in sight, we were amazed to see two youths in the front. We began to run towards the car, shouting as we did. Just as we almost reached the car, they started to pull away — they were stealing it. My heart was racing. Tony noticed that the guy who was driving had wound down the window. As quick as a flash, Tony was running alongside the car and made a dive into the open window, making a grab for the steering wheel. The car was still moving, with Tony hanging out of the window. It veered left and right as they both struggled to gain control, Tony all the time shouting, "Stop this car!" But the youth paid no heed to Tony's pleas. I was running along the other side of the car, banging on the window. I had no idea how this was going to end. Luckily, there weren't many cars about, and, to my great surprise, I saw a young copper running towards us. He was blowing his whistle and shouting for them to halt. When they didn't, he threw — with some force — his big rubber torch at the windscreen. The two youths, startled at this, suddenly stopped the car. The doors flung open and the two made good an escape, the driver losing his jacket to

Mint Vinyl

Tony's grip in the process. The copper gave chase, but they were just too fast.

Moments later, the young copper returned to the car park gasping for breath. "Just couldn't get close enough to grab them!" he exclaimed. He then went on to say, after catching his breath, that he had been in the vicinity because of a number of similar incidents. He then introduced himself, "PC Ian Parker." He looked to be in his early 20s. He continued, "I shall be needing a statement from you, gentlemen. Could I have your names please?" Tony spoke up, telling the officer his name and address, adding that it was his car that they had tried to steal. Then the constable turned to me, "And you are?"

After I gave the constable my name, Tony said, "Jack's just a good friend, I'll give you a statement." He added that he thought that the jacket the would-be thief had left in the struggle might help clear things up. He handed it to PC Parker, who looked through the pockets and found a leather wallet. Inside was a pound note, one ten-shilling note, and some folded pieces of paper. He didn't say what was on them — addresses, I think. But then, in that back of the wallet, he found an ID card. The would-be thief's name was a Mr Simon Mitchell, a local whose address was given as 27 Russel Street. PC Parker put the wallet back into the jacket pocket and addressed Tony, "I will need you to come to the station sometime today if you will, Mr Hibbert." After Tony

A Trip Out

said that he would, PC Parker went back to the police station to make his report.

Now reunited with Janette and Lucy, they enquired how we were after our little incident. For my part, I felt a bit queasy — shock I supposed. Just how Tony was, I couldn't really tell. Just how would you feel after hanging out of a car like that being driven along? Anyway, we talked it over between the four of us, Tony saying that he was okay. I thought he might feel a bit different about it later. We got back into the car and drove to the local nick, following PC Parker's directions. When we arrived, Tony went in to give a statement. He was gone for about 45 minutes, during which time, the three of us talked about what had happened. On reflection of it all, seeing the funny side of things — namely, Tony with his legs hanging and swinging out of the car — I felt sure that later on Tony would be amused at it all. Not really what you expect going out for a nice drive to the park and the zoo. After all that, I resolved to expect the unexpected — you just don't know what might happen. On his return to the car, Tony was already wearing a big grin. When he got in, he said, "What about all that then? We all looked at each other and just roared with laughter. You can't help but see the funny side, can you? We drove back to the hotel and had a lovely meal.

The next day, after Breakfast, we said our goodbyes to Mr and Mrs Collins, thanking them for a most wonderful stay. After loading up the car, we were ready for our home-

Mint Vinyl

ward journey. Not far from the hotel, we had to stop at some traffic lights. In front of us was a little old lady in a Ford Anglia. The lights were on red, then red and amber, then green. We remained motionless during this time. The lights then went back to red, to which I, without thinking, made the remark, "Come on, luv, give us a break. Haven't you seen a colour that you like yet?" To which Lucy piped up, "You do say some strange things, Uncle Jack." Once again everyone laughed. The journey back after that was very forgettable, with not much being said — everyone just thinking how good our stay in Blackpool had been. Arriving back at the shop, and finding all was well, I took my bag and made my way home. I said thank you for everything and that I would be back soon.

Getting back to my apartment, I decided to check my phone and my emails. I was eager to see what had been happening on the business front. I was amazed by how many orders I had received for various albums, both by phone and by email, via my website. But what shocked me more than that, was that some of my emails were of a rather nasty disposition, to the effect of, how dare I sell mint condition albums for the prices I was doing. I had always wanted to sell my products at reasonable prices so that lots more people might be able to afford them. I wasn't comfortable thinking that only the rich could buy them. But now it seemed that I had somehow upset the apple cart. There were a good number of these rather distressing emails. I must

A Trip Out

confess that I was really upset by them—feeling sick to my stomach. Who did these people think they were? Trying to rid myself of these negative thoughts, I began putting the orders onto my phone. But, despite my best efforts, my thoughts were still filled with those nasty emails, some of which even went as far as saying that I should watch my back. Suddenly, I remembered that it was back to work tomorrow. That too was not a happy thought. A very restless sleep was to come.

In the morning, I wasn't feeling too much better. I felt like never looking at another email ever again. I went to work, going through the motions. After what seemed like an age, I got back home. After showering, I got changed, and prepared to go to Tony's. I thought being with Tony would make me feel better. I switched on the radio, got the specs, and set the display. In no time at all I was on the towpath. I made my way to the shop and, going in, I was greeted by Tony and Lucy. Immediately Tony said, "Just watch the shop a minute, Lucy, please." Tony then asked me to follow him into the workshop. We got in there and he said, "I have some bad news for you, Jack." My heart sank. *What else could go wrong?* I thought. Tony continued, "Brian Thorpe's been round again a few times looking for you, Jack. Says Rossi wants a word." All kinds of things began to flood my mind. I didn't want to see Dave Rossi, but I didn't want his monkeys to keep coming into Tony's shop either. I resolved to go and see him.

Mint Vinyl

Tony asked if I would like any company, to which I replied, "I'll be okay on my own."

Taking the bull by the horns, I went around right away. When I got in, Kevin Wilson glared at me and said, "In the back." He lifted up the counter and I made my way through.

"Hello, Jack, or whatever your name is," said Rossi.

"Yeah, it's Jack," I replied. I don't know why, but Dave never seemed to believe a word I said.

He said, or rather, growled, "A little bird tells me you've been winning big at other bookies. Well, I want to know how you're doing it see."

I said to him, with as much defiance as I could muster, "Guess I'm just lucky, Dave. Yeah, Lucky Jack, that's what they call me."

"Okay, have it your way." Opening the back door to his office he yelled, "Get out!" As he grabbed my coat and threw me out, a thought flashed through my mind: *That was short and sweet.* How wrong I was. Waiting for me in the back alley was none other than Mr Wilson. He gave me a good going over, bruising my face, splitting my lip, and, when I dropped down, he gave me a kicking, saying, "I really enjoyed that," knocking on the back door and going inside.

I got up and headed back to the Tony's. On getting back, Tony was surprised to see me in such a state. "I should have gone with you," he said. He took me into the house and cleaned me up, asking if I wanted to get the police involved.

A Trip Out

I didn't want that, so I said no, adding that it would only make things worse.

"Tony, I'll go home and rest for a while and think things over," I said. I made my way back home, and thought to myself, *What a day this has turned out to be*. Trouble is as trouble was!

Chapter 9

A Plan of Action

Once home, I took a lovely refreshing shower. I felt the pain from my ribs, looking down I saw the bruises, and in the bathroom mirror I could see my fat lip, bruised face, and the large bruises on my right side. All in all, I had had a good working over. I got dressed and decided to phone in sick. *Not up for work today*, I thought. I made some toast and a brew and sat in the lounge, thinking of what to do next. On the one side, things were really looking up with the orders, but then there were my unresolved problems—both in 2012 and in 1963. *I must formulate a plan*, I thought. The nasty emails would just have to wait for the moment, the most pressing thing was Dave Rossi. I would have to speak to Tony to ask his advice about the situation. I decided to rest my wounds for the day and see what I could come up with. My life had been full on for some time now, and this inactivity was just killing me. But I was feeling worse for wear, so I just had to grin and bear it.

The next day I returned to work—my fat lip having shrunk somewhat. The day passed without incident, no-

Mint Vinyl

body even asking about my bruises. Getting home, I immediately got ready to go to the sixties, and soon enough I was standing on the towpath. I crossed the bridge and made my way to Tony's shop. I went right over to Tony and asked him if we could talk. "Yes, let's go through," said Tony, "Are you feeling any better, Jack? You look really worried."

"Yeah, I am, Tony, but I don't want this whole thing to backfire on you—got to try and defuse the situation. What do you think about me apologising to Dave personally?"

"Worth a shot I guess."

"Well, that's what I'm going to do, Tony." So, off I went to Dave's shop. When I got inside, Mark Stanley was there.

"Look, I don't want any trouble," he said.

"Me neither," I replied, "can I speak with Dave?"

At that moment Dave walked into the shop and gave me an icy glare.

"What have I told you?" he snarled. "Have you got a death wish or something?"

"Look, Rossi, just hear me out. I just want to apologise for everything that has happened. I will stay out of your way—you won't know I'm here. Please can we call it quits now?"

"I told you before, get out of my shop and my sight!" I left not really knowing if I had achieved anything or not. Dave didn't give much away; he was not exactly an open book. Dave is what he is—a very angry nasty man.

A Plan of Action

I returned to Tony's and told him what had happened. "We'll just have to play a waiting game," I said, "but in the meantime, I have lots more orders for you, Tony."

"Let's have a look," he said. Having placed a very big order, I took my leave, telling Tony that I'd see him soon. I walked into town and sat down on a bench. I began to think about the number of discs that I needed to fulfil my orders. *I will have to start visiting other shops*, I thought. I found a phone box and looked through the book, making a note of any record shops. I would have to visit Brenton, Wrenshaw, and even Manchester. I would also have to back a lot more winners at the bookies, only further afield — not anywhere near Mr Rossi. My bank account was looking pretty healthy, but I needed to finance my expansion, so more winners needed — now I had a plan to go forward. *Maybe someday soon I can start making plans for my shop*, I thought. Feeling a little better about things, I headed for home.

Getting back, I found even more orders. This was getting really exciting. I began putting into practice my plan for fulfilling orders, setting the foundation for how I wanted my shop to work. If I got an order and I didn't know the item, I'd research, decide how long I thought it would take to locate it, then contact the client. It differed with each order, but in one week, two weeks, or more, they received a mint condition copy — and that is the reason people were prepared to wait. Over those few weeks, I was just literally run off my feet, travelling to the past and back to fulfil my orders. So much so, that, for the first time, it all really started to get to me. Even though I had the luxury of being able to set the displays to go and come back at whatever time I chose, I lost track of where I was up to with things and began to make lots of mistakes. I was getting so confused, and not least of my problems was that I was just absolutely worn out. I didn't even know what day it was. Going to work, travelling back; even Tony had asked to speak with me, saying that I just didn't seem myself these days. Things had gotten so bad back home that my doctor had prescribed me some sleeping pills. 21st century living was getting me down.

    I decided to book three days off work and go back to sixty-three. I found a one-bedroom flat to let, over a newsagents in town. I stayed there, just sleeping, and constantly thinking. I also took some walks, but I didn't visit Tony. I felt that I needed to get my head straight. After my break, I was feeling somewhat refreshed. I looked at all my orders and got everything on my phone— another phone I had bought just for all my dates and times etc. I was determined to get organised, so that everything would be manageable. *It's a big ask, but I feel I can do it*, I thought.

    I returned to 1963, setting the displays for two weeks after my last visit. Tony and Lucy were really pleased to see me. Tony remarked that I was looking better—I felt it too. *I've really turned a corner*, I thought. Tony had most of my orders fulfilled, so that was good news. Tony also told me

A Plan of Action

that it was, "All quiet on the Rossi front, no visits, no nothing." Tony then invited me for tea later, to which I accepted. It was good to spend time catching up with friends. Going back with my stock I thought to myself, *I will have some more satisfied customers back home.* I had also been busy with my betting. It was just so good to know that I couldn't lose — unless I wanted to that is. Most of my winnings were deposited in the 'Dansford Mutual Bank'. I chose the bank because it was still in business in 2012, now called 'Dansford Bank'. I'd invested some money in 1963 and got a very healthy return in 2012.

The time was coming for taking a giant leap. I felt like Neil Armstrong — but there was another six years to go before that. I began to make my plans for the shop, and in the meantime continued with my very full life: my clients, my betting, and my friendship with Tony, Janette, and Lucy — we had become inseparable. I was still going to the darts with Tony and the gang, but only to play warm up games. They remained the highlight of my life.

One day, I was invited to tea by Janette. "Of course, I'll come," I said, knowing nothing of her plan. I arrived at about 6pm as usual.

Lucy let me in, saying, "Go through, Uncle Jack." Janette was in the lounge, and to my great surprise there was this very pretty woman in there talking to her.

"Jack, this is April. April, this is Jack." From the very start, I was really struck with April. She had long dark hair,

Mint Vinyl

blue eyes, rosy cheeks, and a wonderful complexion. She was about five foot six, tall, slim, and very friendly. I didn't know at the time, but apparently Janette thought that I needed a good woman in my life. I found out later that she worked at the laundry with Janette, but in the office. So, that was the start of another chapter in my life. Some people might say another distraction in my already complicated life, but she was a very beautiful one. It wasn't long before we became more than just good friends — going out for dinner, the movies, for a drink — we even borrowed Tony's car a couple of times to take a trip out. April became a wonderful part of my life. All that I was missing in 2012 was right there in 1963, and I was so glad.

The business continued to expand, with more and more orders coming in. The nasty emails continued as well, but, fortunately, less frequently. It was becoming very clear that I would have to make a decision about opening up my shop very soon. I had decided to try to rent a place to begin with, so I started my search. Shops on the high street were finding business very tough going at that moment. I came across a hardware shop with a notice in the window that read, 'Looking for someone to share the premises.' I walked in to find that the shop was owned by a husband-and-wife team — Robert and Lindsay Green. I spoke to them about the shop, setting out my plan. They in turn informed me of their plan to downsize their business. We talked it over and decided that we could help each other out. They would get a

A Plan of Action

contract made up, and I would take over half of the shop. It wasn't the largest of places, but it was a start. Now was the time for action.

The whole week after work was spent getting everything ready. I worked in the nights preparing the shop. It was very hard work having, as it is, two jobs on the go. My plan was to have the grand opening in two weeks' time, at the beginning of October. When the day finally came around, I was standing outside the shop. It felt so good to be there. It was hardly an empire, but at last I had my shop. 'Mint Vinyl' was born on Thursday the 4th of October 2012. The shop was in a good location on the corner of the high street and Milton Street in Dansford. I looked at the shop sign, it was an LP with 'Mint Vinyl' written on it in a lovely shade of green. I was there in good time to open up at 9am that morning. To say that business was slow would be an understatement. The hardware store was doing more trade than me, and they were supposedly struggling for business. I counted just six people in the shop all day. What a great start to my dreams. However, I was cheered up by one customer who came in. He enquired if I could get for him the album *Lord Offaly* by David McWilliams. It was an album from 1972 and was also a personal favourite of mine. Talking to him about it cheered me up to no end. Despite not making even one sale, it had been rewarding. I smiled and thought to myself, *Things can only get better.*

Mint Vinyl

I set out a few simple guidelines for the shop that I would use from then onwards. Namely, I didn't want to be like most places, seemingly wanting to know every detail about the customers. All I required was that they took up free membership with the shop. In turn — they would get a little plastic card with 'Mint Vinyl' on one side and a barcode on the other. No names unless they wanted me to know — then only first names. Also, the shop would work like this: I would have small plastic sheets in the rack, each with a photo of an album, and the artist's name written on it. These would have a bar code on them, linked to the shop computer. When one was brought to the counter, it would be zapped and recorded to the customer's membership number. They would then be told how long it would take to acquire the record or records. Payment would be made by card or cash — that was the deal.

In the coming months, it proved to work very well indeed. It all started with just me in the shop, opening only at the weekends. However, I soon realised that I needed help, which came in the shape of two 18-year-old twins — Angela and Rachel Watson. Twins, but as different as chalk and cheese those two. They had responded to my ad in the local paper, and I for one was very glad that they had. They were absolutely fantastic workers, very keen and very trustworthy. Now my shop was open all week, and what's more was doing really well.

A Plan of Action

The shop went from strength to strength, which in turn meant many more visits to the past. I was continuing to research and made further plans for my business. Going back to see Tony was easy if I needed to go back close to our first meeting, but much more difficult if it needed to be further on. I had given this a great deal of thought, and always arrived at the same conclusion — sooner or later, I would have to tell Tony the truth about my travels. I felt that keeping it secret for any longer would be a betrayal of our friendship. *But just how would he take what I would have to say?* I thought. I agonised over this for some days to come. Meanwhile, I had stepped up my betting, placing bets anywhere I could find, and where I thought I would be out of the way of Dave Rossi. My bank balance and my investments were still growing nicely.

My shop was doing well, which was great, but it also caused somewhat of a problem in and of itself. It seemed that the two businesses were complimenting each other. People who came to the hardware shop were also buying at 'Mint Vinyl' and vice versa. One day, the owners of the shop, the Greens, asked for a meeting. Later that day we met in a local coffee shop. They said that they would like all of their shop back, as we were close to the end of our contract. I knew where they were coming from, so I agreed that I would have to find a new premises, and very soon. I had one month in which to sort things out. After looking at estate agents, the local papers, and on the net, I eventually came up with a suitable place not too far away from my present location. It was a larger premises, however, this time I would be buying and not simply renting—it would really be mine. The Greens agreed to put up notices informing people of the move, and I employed a local firm of builders to sort out the shop before the end of my contract.

When all was ready, there was a grand opening. I managed to secure the services of a local radio DJ to do the opening. Lots of people turned up, and it was a rather good event. I was just so pleased that my dreams were at last being fulfilled. I just felt on top of the world. After forgetting all about having to tell Tony about my visits to the past, my head began to swim with thoughts again. But, for the time being, everything was going really well, and it was not long before some more staff were added to the shop. Two guys this time, good friends of the lovely twins Angela and Rachel—Paul and David Cook. Yeah, they were twins also. They all wore their new uniforms, and now in the shop we had music from the sixties and seventies playing. I also had plans to build a small coffee bar in there, but that was a plan for the future.

Chapter 10

Bold Decision

I had brought myself to a place mentally where I felt that I could tell Tony about my life, and all that had happened. I wanted Tony and his family to continue to be an important part of my life. Of course, that would also mean I would have to tell April all about myself. It was time for my bold decision to be executed. Returning to Tony's just after our last meeting, I asked him if I could meet with everybody. I felt that they should all hear it from me. *Just how will they react?* I thought to myself. I would just have to wait and see. I was to go to tea the next day with April after work.

We had a lovely meal as usual. Afterwards, I said, "I have something very important to tell you all about myself. When I do, you will probably thing me mad or something. But it's all true, every last word of it. Here goes." I then related everything to them, starting with my dreams, and then Uncle George's letters, and everything that had happened. It all seemed so surreal; I couldn't believe what I was doing. After I finished speaking, everyone was just speechless.

Mint Vinyl

"How can it be?" said Tony eventually. I had tried to anticipate what their reaction might be, so I took along my tablet. I had some music videos on it and some movies.

"You like electronics, Tony" I said, "well, what's your thoughts on this?" I lay the tablets on the table.

"I've never seen anything like it," said Tony. "Just what is it?"

"Look, I'll show you." Switching it on, I found a music video of the Stones: *It's All Over Now* — Tony, like me, likes the Stones. "Watch this, Tony," I said. He was simply amazed, picking up the tablet and putting in back down, just staring at it as if in a sort of trance. After this I showed them a movie: *Spiderman*. After a few minutes, I asked, "What do you think now about what I have told you?" They all said that they were finding it hard to come to terms with it, but that they had to admit that they did believe me. I said, "Look, I want us to remain best friends, I just thought that I had to tell you. All this doesn't have to make any difference." I then said to everyone, "Look, I'll go now and come back tomorrow. I'll give you all time to think." I made my way home, feeling some doubt about my decision to tell everyone. I still wanted to be able to visit them any time I wanted. *Tomorrow I will find out for sure*, I thought.

Returning to Tony's shop with very mixed emotions, I opened the door and walked in. I was amazed to receive my usual friendly welcome. "How do you feel now about what I had to say?" I asked.

Bold Decision

"You know what you mean to us all, Jack," said Tony.

"Yes, Uncle Jack," added Lucy, "we think the world of you."

"It was a shock," said Tony, "but we know now, and we'll take it from there." But Tony had some bad news for me—Rossi's posse had been in the shop again. Not asking for me this time, but for protection money for the shop. Apparently, this was one of Dave Rossi's little enterprises—terrorising local businesses into paying for protection or face damage to their property. Tony had flatly refused, after which Wilson and co. said that they would return. I had not been in the shop for half an hour when, suddenly, large bricks smashed through the front windows. No prizes for guessing who was behind it all—Rossi!

During the next few days, the posse made several visits to Tony's, always with the same result—Tony would not be paying. Returning to the shop a few days later, I found that a petrol bomb had been thrown through the window. This only caused minor damage, but it was an escalation even so. "Is this going to end?" I said to Tony. "As much as I don't like Rossi, or his methods, wouldn't it be better to get him off your back?" I urged Tony, against his better judgement, to just pay up. Tony at least said that he would consider it. Later, Tony said that he just couldn't do it. He just couldn't pay money to the man he calls, 'that thug'. I wasn't too happy about his decision, but I could at least understand it—I was just very concerned about what would happen next. Well, I didn't have to wait that long to find out.

Tony and I went to visit one of Tony's contacts about some imports. We arrived back at the shop to find the place empty, with Lucy nowhere to be seen. However, what we did find sent shivers down our spines: a note saying:

If you want her back then pay up!

Now things had gone from bad to worse. I asked Tony if we were going to inform the police. "Let's just sit and think about it first," he replied. "Let's put our heads together." Tony had a double worry—for his daughter and also for his wife. "She will be hysterical," he said.

"Where do you think that they'll be holding her?" I asked.

"Not at the shop, that would be too easy. Rossi has lots of lock ups all over the place—for all his ill-gotten gains. My bet is she'll be in one of them. Trouble is, I don't know the whereabouts of them all."

"You've given me an idea, but I will have to return home to put it into action. I'll be back as soon as possible."

"Okay, Jack, thank you."

"I know that you will... but try not to worry too much."

I went back to the present to visit an electronics place I knew. I needed to buy a small radio transmitter and a receiver so we could bug Dave Rossi's car. I got what I needed and went back to Tony's and told him my plan. He was hope-

Bold Decision

ful that it would work, and I assured him that I thought it would. We got into Tony's car and drove to Rossi's shop. Sure enough, Rossi's car was parked outside. I sneaked up to it and, after putting the bug behind the back bumper, went back to Tony's car. "What now?" asked Tony.

"Drive away out of sight," I replied, "then we just wait. He will lead us to her, and we can get her back safely." We both sat in the car, waiting very impatiently for Mr Rossi to visit Lucy. We waited for over an hour and then, suddenly, Rossi was in his car about to set off. He drove around lots of streets, checking to see if he was being followed. We had the luxury of being able to keep well back—we had his signal loud and clear. Eventually, he drove to his lock up. He went in for about ten minutes, then he got back into his car a drove off. We waited for a few minutes, thinking that he might come back. He didn't, so we got some bolt cutters from the boot, and in no time at all Lucy was free, and we headed back to Tony's shop. She had not been hurt by her ordeal but was very shaken up.

Mr Rossi will be furious when he goes back to check on her, I thought. The three of us decided that it would be much better if Janette knew nothing about the abduction. We then talked over what we felt Rossi's next move would be. I said to Tony, "Let me see if I can devise a plan to sort our Mr Rossi once and for all."

I made my way back home in order to formulate what we could do next. I checked my phone messages and my

Mint Vinyl

emails—yet more orders. I also visited my shop—things had been very busy there also. But there was one worrying development that had me very concerned. Apparently, we had received a visit from the local police. They wanted me to call in to the station. I had a card from the police, left by a Detective Constable Robert Fuller. *I suppose I'd better go see what it is that they want to speak to me about,* I thought.

I arrived at the station, and spoke to the desk sergeant Mike Wilde, a tall thick set guy, dark hair, clean shaven, looked very fit, and probably worked out, mid-thirties I would say. He told me to take a seat and that he would call DC Fuller. I sat and waited and, about two minutes later, DC Fuller appeared. "Mr Roberts," he said.

"That's right," I replied, "Jack Roberts."

"I understand you have a shop just off the high street, on Alton Street in fact. Is that correct, sir?"

"It is," I replied. He then escorted me to an interview room. "Do you mind explaining what this is all about?" I asked.

"Certainly, Mr Roberts. We have had several requests to look into your business."

"What do you mean?"

"Well, do you mind telling me your suppliers of your albums, sir?"

I quickly responded by saying, "Why do you need to know that? I can assure you everything is legal and completely above board."

Bold Decision

"Well, you won't mind telling me who it is then will you, sir." At this point my mind was racing, I thought to myself that this must be an escalation of the nasty emails I had been receiving.

"Look, Detective Fuller," I said, "I have lots of contacts based all over the country. You can check any of my records, everything is in order."

"Some names would be a step forward if you don't mind, sir." I agreed and named some contacts I had done business with. Tony's name did not appear for obvious reasons. I just couldn't believe how some people could be so vindictive when all I wanted to do was be fair and honest with people. DC Fuller left with the names, telling me that he would be in touch.

Going back home, I reflected on all that had been transpiring. Things were getting very complicated. I decided to visit Tony to check on how things were going in '63. I also wanted to see April. Since our first meeting at Tony's, I had not been able to get her out of my mind. I began to realise that I was in love. When I returned to Tony's shop, all seemed well. Tony then told me, "Dave Rossi has been in on two occasions, demanding money for protection, and also asking after you."

After spending some time with Tony discussing all of this, I said, "Just leave it with me. I will come up with a plan." Taking my leave, I went to visit April. Just seeing her pretty face and being in her company made me forget all of my recent troubles. She had such a wonderful nature—I had never met anyone quite like April. We went for a meal and just made some small talk. I told her a little of how I felt about her. She then gave me a big and said, "I know, I feel the same way about you too, Jack." We arranged to meet the next day, and after walking her home I returned home myself.

After making myself a snack and a good strong cup of tea, I began to write down a few thoughts about what we could do about Rossi. I thought, *What we need to do is turn the tables on him — give him something to think about instead.* Tony had told me lots about Rossi's activities, so I thought that we would need to spoil a few of them. I devised a plan that involved a large ring, bearing the skull and crossbones. Tony had told me that Rossi had a fascination with all things pirate. I looked around at various second-hand shops and pawnshops and the like, and eventually turned one up. I worked on the ring, placing a small microphone inside it, connected to a receiver. Now all we needed was a little cunning on our part. The ring would fit very nicely into our plan, as I knew Dave Rossi loved bling — especially something like this. *He won't be able to resist it,* I thought. *It will just fit his persona; he sees himself as some modern-day pirate.*

When everything was ready to go, I travelled back to Tony's, telling him of my scheme. We needed Tony to visit Dave's betting shop on the pretext of discussing the protection money. Taking the ring, Tony went to Dave asking him for a little more time, to which Rossi replied, "Two days more, then cough up!" Before leaving, Tony left the ring in

Bold Decision

the shop and got out quickly to hide outside and watch. Robert Brown found the ring and was busy admiring it when, suddenly, Dave Rossi spotted him with it. Snatching it from his hand, he held it up to the light and gave a very unaccustomed grin. He placed it on his finger—it was as if it was made for him. The plan was in action!

After a good few days of listening to what, quite frankly, was waffle from Dave Rossi and his posse, we heard just what we had been waiting for—a job was being planned. They were going to hijack a shipment of cigarettes on Thursday, then being Tuesday. The plan was to see which lock-up Dave would store his booty in—then we would tip off the police. We knew that Dave rented these lockups under false names, and always paid cash, and never himself.

Thursday came around, and we followed from a safe distance. Dave and co. took the cigarettes to the lock-up on Allen Street. Now all that remained was the tip-off. Dave was not going to be a happy camper next time he visited the lock-up. I just wish I would have been there to see the look on his face. What made this all seem so much better was the fact that it was Dave himself who gave us the nod. It was too dangerous to be present, and we were not really all that welcome at the shop, so just our imagination would have to suffice.

We were able to repeat this process on various occasions over the next few weeks. After a couple of weeks Dave Rossi himself paid Tony a visit, asking if he knew anything about what was going on. Tony said that he knew nothing about

Dave's business interests and, quite frankly, that he didn't want to. Rossi didn't mention protection, as he was obviously too taken up with his goods being repossessed. Tony told me that Dave looked really worried and very nervous when he came into the shop. It was all beginning to get to our mutual friend Dave Rossi. Tony and I agreed that this was great news... well at least for us it was. Dave would think that someone was the snitch — little did he know that is has himself who was the snitch.

Back home, things were still going from strength to strength. We were getting so many orders from the shop it was unbelievable. At this rate, I knew that I would have to start considering going full time. It was getting very hard juggling work and my many trips. Although I had some great help in the shop, it was me who had all the logistics to take care of, and it was beginning to take a toll on me. Upon returning home, it was taking hours to process the orders. Although I could go and return to any time I wished, I was still getting physically and mentally drained. I had come to the conclusion that something had to change — work would have to go.

I informed my employer that I would be leaving. I didn't think that anyone would miss me too much anyway. I was practically invisible there, with no real friends to speak of. Anyway, that done, I now at least would have some more breathing space to get on with the fulfilment of my dreams. Although I must confess it was proving much harder to get

Bold Decision

there than I had imagined. I was still placing lots of bets on the horses and dogs, I had even thought about winning the pools, *But we'll see about that on*e, I thought. I was still banking my winnings and my balance was really handsome now, both in the past and also in the present.

After a while of not hearing back from the police, DC Fuller called into the shop and told me that they had made some inquiries and at the moment they were satisfied that my business was legitimate. Well at least that was a weight off my mind. It had been hard enough to tell Tony and everyone the truth about my travels. I couldn't imagine telling DC Fuller, *He'd want to lock me up and throw the key away*, I thought, chuckling to myself.

It wasn't too long before I realised that I would have to open another shop to cope with the demand for mint vinyl. I consulted with my employees in a meeting after work one evening. They said they had friends who would be very interested in working in the shop. I told them that I would look for suitable premises, and they could get the new staff and see to their training. *I don't know where I would be without my staff*, I thought. I did try to do my part by paying a good wage and providing good working practices and conditions. I eventually found a good size shop further down the high street. I managed to employ the shop fitter again, and, in a matter of weeks, we were ready to open. No big opening this time, as by now lots of people were aware of 'Mint Vinyl' and its services. We had a good reputation now, no small part due to my staff. The new shop would be staffed by a young man called Peter Bradshaw, and a young lady called Kathrine Harris, both good friends of my other staff members.

The shops were both going great guns, which in turn meant plenty of visits to the past. To say that things were hectic is an understatement — it was just complete and utter madness. Sometimes when I sat and thought about things it hardly seemed possible. My dreams were being lived out, but I had never imagined it being so stressful. It was good now that Tony was in the picture about my trips. As a result, I was free to visit him any time to purchase the records that I needed to fulfil my many orders. Without Tony and his family, my dreams would never have found fulfilment. Also, meeting April, and the way I was feeling about her, had changed my whole outlook on life so very much. But with the great success of my business came the negative side of things. The logistics were just so complicated, sometimes making my head feel like it was about to explode. I decided that I would speak to Tony about taking a break away somewhere. I really needed to recharge the batteries.

Chapter 11

A Trip to the Lakes

I went to see Tony, arriving at the shop just before closing. I asked Tony if we could talk, and we went into the house. I asked Tony how he would feel about taking a break and suggested that we go to the lakes. Tony and Lucy were thrilled with the idea, and when Janette got home from work, she also agreed that it was a great idea. Now I just needed to see April to get her opinion. April also thought it would be great, adding that she had never been to the lakes before. I then said, "Okay then, leave the details with me." And so, with great excitement and anticipation, I made a trip to the tourist information bureau, getting some numbers and details of some cottages in the lakes. I decided on an eight-berth cottage in Ambleside, owned by a couple by the name of Frank and Julie Taylor. It looked like a lovely place from the picture. I contacted them and made all the arrangements. We would leave in three days' time and travel up in Tony's car.

The day arrived—Saturday morning—and we all arrived at Tony's place bright and early. Everyone was very excited. Tony's friend was looking after the shop, and I had told my employees that I would be away for a few days, as I planned to let some time elapse in the present while I was in the past so that I would arrive back on the present's next Monday. I knew they would have no trouble coping without me there — I had total confidence in their abilities. The car was all packed up and we all piled in. The time had come, and we were off. The journey would be quite a bit longer than it was in 2012, but it was great that I was with the people that I loved most. We passed through some lovely countryside on the way to Lancaster, then Kendal, Windermere, and then on up to Ambleside. The journey was long, but lots of fun. Finally, we arrived at Hilltop cottage, where we were met by our hosts the Taylors. After our introductions, it was obvious that we were going to be good friends with Frank and Julie. Frank was a good-looking guy — brown hair, blue eyes, and about five foot ten. Julie was about five foot — very pretty, with long natural blonde hair and a wonderful complexion. They were both so very bubbly and very friendly — we hit it off right from the start. Frank and Julie also had a daughter — seven years old, by the name of Katy — very polite and helpful and a credit to her mum and dad. She was also very pretty, with blue eyes, and hair just like her mum. After we got settled into the cottage, we were invited to the farmhouse to see Frank and Julie. We spent a lovely evening with the Taylors — such a great couple. We talked and laughed long into the night, eventually making our way back to the cottage.

A Trip to the Lakes

After a good night's sleep, we awoke to a beautiful day. We enjoyed a good breakfast, and then spent some time sorting out our clothes and other stuff. The cottage was very nice, in fact it was immaculate. I could see that a lot of time and effort had gone into everything in there—the matching furniture, the TV and radio, and a lovely wood-burning stove for any cold nights. We all felt very relaxed and at home, and our hosts were just brilliant. The day was spent mostly in play with Lucy, Tony, Janette, and of course April. We also did some reading—just an all-round relaxing day.

In the evening we invited the Taylors for a meal at a local restaurant. I paid the bill, telling everyone, "It's my treat for having such good friends." During the meal we discussed our plans for the following day. It was decided that we would visit Lake Windermere to take a boat trip.

The next day we set off about 10am for Windermere. When we first arrived, we walked around and went into some of the gift shops and bought a few souvenirs of our trip. Later we all had something to eat together, and then headed off for our boat trip. Once on board, we started to relax and take in the breath-taking scenery. Young Katy seemed to be having a whale of a time—it looked like she was in dream land. Her imagination must have been running wild. People were chatting and pointing in various directions, the sun was shining, and the sky was blue—what a glorious day. Then, out of nowhere, Katy, who must have been lost in play, fell overboard. Tony and I saw it happen and we both instinctively dived into the lake. Luckily the lake was like a mill pond. Tony reached her first and held on to her, while I franticly waved at the boat disappearing away from us. There were people pointing and shouting that people had gone overboard. By this time the Taylors were franticly looking at the lake towards their daughter. Amidst all the shouting, the crew had now realised what was happening and sent out a small boat to pick us up. We got into the boat and wrapped a blanket around Katy, who was now crying uncontrollably. It had been quite a day for the young lady. We got back into the boat and Katy was reunited with her parents. They lavished lots of kisses on her and then began to thank Tony and me. We just said that we were glad that we saw it happen quickly enough. Who would have thought at the start of such a beautiful day that there would be so much drama?

    When we reached the shore, the captain asked the Taylors for their address and so forth, adding that he would have to inform the police and his company of what had happened, and to expect a visit from the police and a representative from the company. We all decided to cut short our outing so that we could all get Katy back home. So, we all piled back into the Taylors' mini-van and drove back to the cottage and farmhouse. Frank and Julie invited us to a meal at the farmhouse for later that evening. We enjoyed a very nice meal together — Julie being and exceptional cook. Katy went to bed early, still feeling rather shaken up by the events of the day. Frank and Julie thanked us once again, we just said that

A Trip to the Lakes

anyone would have done the same. I thought that we had already become good friends, but this incident seemed to have cemented our friendship even further. We talked and drank wine long into the night. Frank and Julie were such a wonderful couple. We were all so glad we had decided to come to Ambleside. These were perhaps not the circumstances I would have chosen to develop a lasting friendship, but I guess sometimes things just overtake us. When we all finally got to bed, we slept quite well considering our day.

I was awake fairly early the next day, so I decided to make a start on breakfast. I made bacon, eggs, sausage, beans, and toast, with tea and coffee. Everyone was pleasantly surprised when they began to rise. Tony said, "Listen, people think that we were some kind of heroes or something, Jack, but I don't see it that way."

"Me neither," I said, "but what can we do? It was just instinct." After a great breakfast, we called on Frank and Julie to see how Katy was doing.

Frank opened the door and said, "Come in." We asked about Katy. Then Frank said, "See for yourselves." She was happily playing with her dolls.

"Well, that's good to see, Frank," I said. I then said to the Taylors that, "We are planning some touring today, taking in a few of the lakes, and maybe even a little walking." Frank told us that he and Julie were staying in with Katy. We told them that that was fine, and we took our leave.

Mint Vinyl

Getting back to the cottage, we got out a map and decided on the details of our trip. We had a great discussion about where to visit, each of us having a different lake that we wanted to see. We decided that we would take in Coniston Water, Ullswater, Buttermere, and Derwentwater. Our day was very full, and quite tiring. We arrived back at the cottage really late—at least much later than we had planned. As we arrived home, I thought to myself, *I won't need to be rocked to sleep tonight*. We were all truly exhausted and trundled off to bed saying our goodnights.

I was awake early and got some coffee on and made some toast and poured myself some orange juice from the fridge. Soon I was joined one by one by Tony and Janette, then April, and finally by Lucy. We all sat around the breakfast table, relating our trip the previous day. There was much talk and lots of laughter—it had been a great day, the memories of which would stay with me for a lifetime. I couldn't help but think of the people around me then as anything but my family. I was feeling so happy, and all my problems and troubles seemed very distant in this atmosphere of, to me, family life. Finally, and with great reluctance, I said to Tony, "Later today we will have to be heading home."

Tony replied, "Listen, let's tidy up the place, get packed up, go see the Taylors, then grab some lunch by the lakeside, taking in the view one last time."

A Trip to the Lakes

"Sounds like a plan to me," at which, for some strange reason, everyone burst into fits of laughter, I couldn't imagine why!

Once ready, we called on our friends Frank and Julie, and of course Katy. They appeared to be sad to see us leave. We told them how good it had been, adding that they had been wonderful hosts, that we wished to remain friends, and that we felt a real connection with them. Frank spoke up — there seemed to be tears in his eyes — he said, "We will miss you so much. We feel we have known you for so long, not just a few days." We shook hands and gave lots of hugs and told the Taylors that we would keep in touch. We went to the car and waved goodbye as we made our way home.

On the journey home Janette said how much she had enjoyed our stay with the Taylors. I hadn't felt this good in years. April said to me, "If it's possible, I'd like to go back sometime, just the two of us."

"That would be fantastic," I said, "I would love to do that." On our way back we spent some time looking at the scenery and spotting blue cars, red cars — you name it we spotted it.

Finally, reaching Tony's place, we took out our luggage and April and I said our goodbyes to Tony, Janette, and Lucy. April and I walked to April's place, where I gave her a passionate kiss, and told her, "April, I want you to know I'm very much in love with you."

She looked into my eyes and said, "Me too, Jack, me too."

Mint Vinyl

"See you soon," I said. I then began to make my way home. I went past Tony's once again and on to the canal towpath, and as I reached the spot, I began to wonder what awaited me in the future. I touched my specs and brought up the display. I consulted my notepad and set the display accordingly.

I was back in the lounge of my apartment, three days after I had left. As I opened the door, sitting on the mat was my mail: some bills, some junk, and two letters in white envelopes, handwritten with local postmarks. I was intrigued, and separated these two from the rest, placing them on my coffee table. After going into the kitchen and putting on a jug of coffee, I picked up one of the letters, opened it up, and took out a note, finding that it was from a man called Phillip Johnson, who it seemed was in the same line of business as myself. He wrote that he lived in Brenton, where he had a shop, and that he would like to meet with me to discuss some things. In his letter, he asked if we could meet at 'The Monk' — it being one of those rather trendy wine bars. Not my ideal choice of venue, but that's what he wanted. I must admit to being quite puzzled by his letter as he made no mention of what he had in mind — my mind was working overtime as to what that might be. The proposed meeting was on Thursday evening, so there was not that long to wait. He had given me his email address to confirm the time or propose another. I emailed him to confirm my attendance on Thursday, to which I received a short and to the point reply.

A Trip to the Lakes

Placing the first letter down, I picked up the second — this one seemed very different. The writing on the envelope was far neater, and I couldn't help but notice a wonderful aroma coming from the envelope. *This must be from a woman,* my mind immediately said, *but who could it be?* Women, as a general rule, didn't write letters to me — at least not in the current time. So, with some excitement, I opened the envelope, finding that the letter, like the envelope, was immaculately written. The letter was from a Miss Phillipa Richards. I was amazed to find out that she was in my class at school, and that she now lived in Sansfield. I tried to picture her, but just couldn't seem to. I rushed to my bedroom, searching for my old photos I kept in a box in there. I grabbed the box and returned to the lounge. I rummaged through the photos and found a school picture of my class. Looking at it, I wondered just which one of the girls was Phillipa. Luckily for me, everyone's names were printed on the back. It had been years since I had looked at this photograph, and I could only remember a few of the faces I saw before me. Finding where Phillipa was on the picture, I stared at it for quite some time. She was a pretty girl, very petite, and fresh faced. My mind wondered what she looked like in the present, and what she could want with me after all these years.

Reading on, she asked if we could meet up, writing that she had a business proposition to put to me, and adding that she would love to see me again. She gave me her mobile number and asked for me to call to set something up.

Chapter 12

The Meeting

It seemed only polite not to keep a lady waiting, so I picked up my phone and dialled Phillipa's number. It started to ring, my heart began to beat faster, my hands were becoming sweaty, I thought, *What is happening to me?* Then I heard the voice of a woman say, "Hello." The voice was very quiet and sounded very refined.

I replied, "Is that Phillipa?"

She said, "Yes, it is."

"Jack Robert's here, you wrote to me."

"Yes, I did, Jack. May I call you Jack."

"Of course."

"It's so good to speak to you, Jack. Please could we meet up somewhere?"

"Of course. Do you know 'The Lantern' restaurant in town?"

"Yes, I do."

"Could we meet there on Tuesday evening at 7pm?"

She agreed and said, "See you soon, Jack."

Mint Vinyl

Ending the call, I found myself to be very elated about getting in touch with Phillipa after so long. My mind was very preoccupied with what her business plan might be. However, I needed to bring myself back to the here and now. I knew that I must pay a visit to my shops to check up on things. Three days had elapsed since I was in my shops before setting out to the past—it now being Monday, having left on a Friday. I checked my phone and went online to check the website. It had been inundated with orders. Once more, my head began to swim with the thoughts of the logistical nightmare that lay ahead. When I had first dreamt of opening the shop, I had been tremendously excited by the prospect of meeting like-minded people, discussing albums with them, and seeing their faces when they received their mint copies of their choice. Now all of that had disappeared. I was now so involved in the fulfilment of the orders, there seemed to be little time left for anything else. On checking my phone again, I realised that I had again received several nasty comments about my business. Some of them seemed to border on the verge of, dare I say it, 'Hatred!'

With these thoughts running around my mind, I made my way to the first shop. I reached the shop and entered to see lots of customers browsing—some at the counter, and some talking to staff. When there was something of a lull, I got a chance to speak to Angela and Rachel, with Sam and David still busied by customers. I was greeted by big beaming smiles. Angela said, "So good to see you, Mr Roberts."

The Meeting

"It's Jack, Angela," I said.

"Sorry, Mr Roberts."

These girls, and lads for that matter, were just naturally very polite, and try as I might, I always seemed to end up being called Mr Roberts. "How have things been while I've been away?"

Rachel replied, "Very good, Mr Roberts. Most of our stock has gone and we have lots of orders."

"Excellent," I replied, "well done all of you. I am so glad to have you."

Checking the orders, the staff had received, I was amazed at how well things were going, but could not help thinking that this just meant more time spent away for me. I loved my trips into the past, especially because of April — the love of my life — and of course my very good friends the Hibberts. However, juggling two separate lives was beginning to feel very difficult to handle.

My visit to the other shop had a similar outcome — many more orders and a great depletion in the stock. There was much preparation to be done before returning to the past. As I made my way back to my apartment focused on all these things, I couldn't help but think that most of my problems stemmed from the fact that so much of my business had to be by very nature one big secret — at least in my time. I thought, *If there was someone in which I could confide in, what a relief it would be — what a weight off my mind to have someone*

Mint Vinyl

to help me with all this pressure. This was not what I wanted the fulfilment of my plans and dreams to be.

After spending hours on logistics, I finally prepared myself a meal and tried to relax somewhat. I settled down after eating with a large tot of rum and listened to some music on my record deck. I listened to my first purchase from the beginning of my adventure—Ol' Blue Eyes himself. The next thing I remember was waking up to silence, with a nasty crick in my neck, and finding an empty tumbler on the floor. I got to my feet and stretched and roamed from room to room, pausing to look out of the window to the towpath. The water was shimmering from the lights from the apartment block and the lights on this stretch of the canal. My mind returned to thoughts of my meeting with Phillipa Richards the next day. I retired to bed with these thoughts still running through my head.

The night was a restless one—I didn't sleep well at all. Finding myself wide awake at 4am, I got up and went to the kitchen to make a mug of coffee. *May as well have a caffeine injection, as sleep is so far away from me anyway,* I thought. I checked my emails again and the messages on my phone. Steering myself away from the somewhat unhelpful messages I was receiving again, I decided to shower and change. Feeling invigorated, I took an early breakfast. It was still early in the morning, so, as I glanced out of my window, I decided to take a stroll.

The Meeting

Going down, I met one person coming out of a ground floor apartment. It was a young lady I had seen before, but I didn't know her name. After sharing a brief hello and good morning with her, I walked onto the towpath. The early morning was a pleasant one — it looked like we could be in for a beautiful day. There were some ducks on the canal, breaking the silence. Even though it was quite loud, there was something rather soothing about it. I gazed around, taking in the view. It was just one of those days when you feel happy to be alive.

After a walk of about twenty minutes, I returned to my apartment, arriving back at 7:20am. I switched on the radio and heard a favourite song of mine: *I Heard It Through the Grapevine*. I usually listened to one of the gold stations playing all the old hits. Unusually, I felt at ease, even though I had this meeting scheduled with Phillipa. I felt completely relaxed about it — I didn't have any anxiety at all, even though I had no idea why she wanted to discuss business. I made a change of clothes and prepared to go and see Tony as there were some things that I really needed to talk to him about regarding lots of the orders I had received.

Making all the necessary preparations, I went back to 1963, setting the time and date for the day after my previous visit. As soon as I arrived at the shop, I sensed an atmosphere. My plans to talk record business would have to go on hold. Tony seemed very agitated and shouted me to follow him into his workshop. Once in there, he produced a

Mint Vinyl

letter from his pocket and handed it to me saying, "Listen, read this. It must be Rossi again. Can't think of anyone else who would want to stir up trouble like this other than that thug." I read the letter—it was from the local council. They were writing that they had received a complaint about an unlicenced business operating on the premises (i.e., electrical repairs). I had never seen Tony so upset as this before. It was probably a culmination of all the other things that Dave Rossi had put him through. Tony was right—he really was a nasty mean thug.

With some difficulty, I managed to calm Tony somewhat, saying, "Let's sit down and talk it through." Tony's main concern was for Janette and Lucy, but they were both very supportive, seeing how upset Tony was about all this, and Janette had taken a day off work to be with him. The three of us went into the lounge and begun to talk it through, while Lucy stayed in the shop.

I asked Tony if he had done anything about it yet, to which he replied, "No."

I said, "This is what I feel we should do. Let's draft a letter to the council asking for permission to operate the repair business from your workshop. Then I suggest that you call them to make an appointment," adding that, if he wished, I would go with him for support. We agreed to do just that.

Janette said, "I will draft the letter. I'll get on it right away."

The Meeting

Just then, Lucy shouted from the shop for her dad to go in. Tony went through to find Dave Rossi himself holding a radio and asking Tony if he could fix it for him. Then, smirking, he said, "Oh no, you can't can you? What a pity you don't have a licence." Needless to say, this did not go down well with Tony, and I had to intervene to physically restrain him from attacking Mr Rossi.

"Get out of my shop," Tony said, "I don't want you or your kind in here." Tony was in a real rage, and it took some time for the three of us to calm him. Also, I must add that I myself didn't escape Mr Rossi's sarcastic tone.

Just before leaving the shop, Mr Rossi had turned around and said, "And as for you, Jack, or whatever your name is, I haven't forgotten about you." My initial thought was simply, *Trouble is as trouble was.* During our conversation with Tony, I apologised for being the cause of at least some of the troubles we found ourselves in.

Tony quickly butted in saying, "Listen, that guy was trouble long before you ever came into my shop. I know that this sounds harsh, but I have a hatred towards that man—he makes my blood boil—and when I see myself when he's around, even I don't like myself."

I replied, "Anyway, make that call to the council and try to set up a meeting. Just let me know when and I'll be here for you—don't worry on that score." I really did need to speak to Tony about my orders, a lot of which were for albums later in the sixties and seventies. I just wanted to square it with him, but it would just have to wait—no pressure!

Speaking with Janette she said, "He'll be alright, we can see to him now and make sure he makes that call." Saying my goodbyes, I made my way back over the bridge and onto the towpath. When no one was around I touched the specs and set the display to arrive back in the early evening, as I didn't want to wait too long between getting back and meeting Phillipa. I needed a distraction from all the negativity, so, getting back into the apartment at around 5pm, I turned on the TV and went to the bedroom to undress and take a shower. That done, I initially dressed casually, as I would change a little later. Going back into the lounge, I glanced at the TV—yet another shooting somewhere. The news was always so depressing—it seemed like the whole world was going mad. Making myself a brew, I switched off the TV and turned on the radio. I settled into my favourite chair and tried not to dwell on the problems of the sixties.

After a short while, I changed into one of my suits and found a nice tie to go with it. I looked in the wardrobe mirror—it looked pretty good even if I say so myself. But as I looked closer, I saw a lot more grey hairs at the sides than I remembered. *The stress must really be getting to me*, I thought. I called a cab and arrived at 'The Lantern' at 6:45pm. It was a very upmarket restaurant situated in the outskirts of town—what people term 'the posh end of town'—on Upper Grange Avenue, lined on both sides by

The Meeting

tall poplar trees. The restaurant had a huge neon sign of a lantern on its frontage, a massive car park, and of course a mostly wealthy clientele. The inside of the restaurant was spectacularly decorated, just oozing with style—somewhat extravagant but I must say I did like going there. I gave my name, adding that I had a reservation. I was escorted to table ten a candlelit table for two—by that I mean there was a lantern on the table containing a very lovely, scented candle. All around were very smartly dressed diners—lots of jewels were on display, worn by many pretty ladies of various ages. At 5 minutes to 7 Phillipa was escorted to the table, and I immediately rose to greet her. I really didn't remember her from school, but before me now was a beautiful woman wearing a lovely blue dress and a sparkling pendant. I glanced at her hands to see she was wearing on ring on her right hand. She said in a very soft voice, "So good to see you, Jack." I was struggling to hear her clearly, so I made a mental not to myself that I must give full attention to her when she was speaking.

I said, "Lovely to see you. I must start by apologising. I'm very sorry, but when I received your letter, I just couldn't place you from our school days at all. Hope that you can forgive me."

"Nothing to forgive, it's been so long."

We ordered drinks—asking the waiter if he would let us order a little later. He said, "As you wish."

Mint Vinyl

Phillipa said, "Well, Jack, I suppose you are a little surprised, maybe even puzzled, by my request to meet with you."

"I must admit to being intrigued. It's not every day you meet up with someone from way back—especially not with a lady as charming and as beautiful as you."

"Oh, you're too kind. I must say you have become a handsome man, Jack. What I'm proposing is this. You may be unaware of my profession. I am a web designer with my own company." She handed me a business card which read: 'Webtastic Superior Web Designs by Phillipa Richards'.

"What does this have to do with me?" I asked.

"Well, Jack, a few days ago I stumbled upon your website and—please bear with me on this—but it's not that professional I'm afraid. I got to thinking that I could do a much better job for you." I felt like she had fired an arrow and punctured my ego—it was well and truly deflated.

Desperately trying to retain some composure, I said, "That's very interesting, but why would you want to do that."

"Three reasons I believe. Firstly, I have a keen interest in collecting vinyl; secondly, I would like very much to buy into your company and be in charge of sales; and thirdly, I wanted so much to meet with you again and form a firm friendship."

"Well, that's a lot to take on board," I replied.

The Meeting

"You don't have to decide here and now, Jack. You have my number."

"I do indeed, and I will be in touch. However, for now let's enjoy a lovely evening together."

We did exactly that. Afterwards I suggested sharing a cab. She said, "Thank you, but there's no need. My chauffer is waiting in the car park."

I smiled and said, "Okay then, I will be in touch. Thank you for such a lovely evening!" She left, I went to the desk to settle the bill, and I called a cab. On the journey home I couldn't help but be impressed by this wonderful lady I had just spent the evening with. Arriving back at the apartment, I went in, took off my jacket, and loosened my tie. Pouring myself a nightcap, I sat down and thought to myself, *Sometimes life can be remarkably good.* Then, like a bolt out of the blue, I came back to earth with a bump when I remembered Tony and all his trouble. I felt responsible for quite a lot of them. I went to bed in a mixture of two things: elation and deflation in equal measures.

I slept well considering my thoughts when retiring. After breakfast I showered and changed, getting ready to go to Tony's—hoping for some good news for once. Having gone through my preparations, I once more found myself standing on the towpath in 1963. The air was fresh and clear today—a little chilly but the sky was bright blue. As I made my way over the bridge towards Tony I couldn't help but notice that there seemed to be more people around than normal.

Lots of them greeted me with, "Good morning." I thought that perhaps people were getting used to seeing me out and about. I was filled with expectancy that there would be some good news today. Reaching the shop and going in, I was pleased to see Tony and Lucy both busy with customers—looking much brighter than when I saw them last.

When there was a lull in the trade Tony said, "Come through."

I followed him saying, "How's things?" but before going in I spoke with Lucy, who gave me a huge smile and a hug. "How are you?" I asked her.

"I'm fine, Uncle Jack."

"You're sure?"

"Yes, I'm doing good, Dad's waiting." She pointed to the open door, and I turned and walked in. Inside, Tony said that after his phone call to the council, they said they would send out a letter in the next couple of days setting up a meeting about licencing the property for electrical repairs.

"That's great," I said.

Tony replied, "Listen, that's just brilliant, not just great." Tony seemed in such good spirits, so I decided to ask him about all the albums I require, stating that I would have to visit him in different years. He grabbed me by both arms and smiled, saying, "Jack, for you anything my friend, anything at all." A strong wave of relief swept over me. It was

The Meeting

so good to see Tony looking and sounding so positive. I said thanks and added that he must let me know when he got word from the local council, as I would be pleased to attend the meeting with him. I set the display to arrive back on Wednesday evening in preparation for my meeting with Phillip Johnson the next day.

Chapter 13

Ultimatum

I now found myself thinking that Thursday's meeting with Phillip Johnson may not go as well as the meeting with Phillipa. I didn't know why, but I already had a strange uneasiness about meeting Mr Johnson. I knew nothing about him except for what he himself had been forthcoming about. I arrived at lunchtime at 'The Monk' to find Mr Johnson already there, seated in an alcove. As I walked over, he raised a hand gesturing to me. I held out my hand to shake, but he made no attempt to reciprocate my actions. I said, "Mr Johnson, I'm Jack, Jack Roberts."

The first words out of his mouth were, "I know who you are. You're the man ruining my business."

"Excuse me, how can that be?" I replied. *This is Mr Negativity himself*, I thought. His whole persona was one of coldness in my direction. He was just oozing dislike for me on a huge scale. I began to think that I was right in my foreboding. I took a seat and he immediately launched into what I can only describe as some kind of pent-up fury towards me.

Mint Vinyl

"What gives you the right to sell mint condition albums for the ridiculous prices that you do?" he said. "My trade has gone down forty percent already. Just who do you think you are?"

I was just reeling from all this. I had never taken such an instant dislike to someone before in my life as to this guy. He was so nasty, bitter, and twisted it's hard to put it into words. Suddenly, it all started to fall into place—*He must be the author of many of my nasty messages*, I thought. I tried in vain to talk to him rationally, but he was having none of it. Seemingly only his point of view counted for anything in this matter. I didn't even have such a bad first encounter with a certain Mr Rossi. Finally, I said, "If you won't allow me to speak to you in a civilised manner, then I don't have any more to say to you, Mr Johnson. I bid you farewell." He glared at me as I rose to leave; his eyes seemed to bore through me.

Spittle flew from his mouth as he said, "I'm giving you an ultimatum, Roberts. Stop what you are doing or else!"

I left visibly shaken by what had taken place. I just needed the comfort and refuge of my apartment at that moment. On my way home my mind was in a fog. I thought, *How can two people be so different?* When I thought of Phillipa, and then Phillip, I just could not comprehend it—what a difference a letter can make! In my lounge, I poured myself a large rum and dropped into my chair.

Chapter 14

Back with Friends

Coming somewhat to my senses, I showered and changed to go and see April—I needed to feel her sweet embrace. After the tirade I received, I needed to be covered with love. Making all the preparations, I arrived at April's, knowing that she would be home from the laundry at that time. I knocked on the door and she answered, looking as radiant as ever. The terrible feelings I had from my meeting seemed to vanish at the sight of her beautiful face and wonderful smile. "Come in, Jack," she said.

"Thank you, I just need to be with you very much." I replied. Once I was in the house, the events of the meeting just poured out of me.

April just cuddled me and kissed my forehead saying, "You have me and Tony and Janette and Lucy. You mean the world to us, Jack."

"I know—and it means so much to me," I said.

Then she said to me, "There is something that I need to talk to you about."

"What's that, my love?"

Mint Vinyl

"I am struggling with you having, as it were, two lives. I love you, Jack—with all my heart—but I just can't get my head around this time travel thing." Once again, my mind was racing, almost like there were cogs and gears whizzing and whirring inside my head. She said, "I just need some time to think." Right then, at that moment, I wished that I was incapable of thinking. It felt like my head was about to explode.

I said my goodbyes to April and made my way to Tony's place to just pop in and see him. No matter what was happening, if my shops were going to be restocked then I needed to make myself get on with things. Going in, I could tell straight away by Tony's body language that he was feeling much brighter. Sure enough, he said "Listen, wonderful news. We have a meeting on Tuesday next week with the council, and I'm feeling good about it."

"That's fantastic," I said, "what time is it for? I might come along if it will be of any help to you." I didn't want to promise Tony that I'd attend anything in future, knowing that I may be meeting Tony after any such promised time to collect albums—and from his point of view I would have not showed up—at least that's what I assumed anyway. *Best to keep things open*, I thought.

"10:30am, Tony answered. "Listen, be here for 10 if you're coming, but only if you're not busy." I then checked about my visits to different time periods. Tony said, "I'll be here." Just before I left, I decided to confide in Tony about

Back With Friends

April. I thought, *Janette will know already and if she doesn't, she soon will* — so, I just thought it best. Laying a hand on my shoulder, Tony said, "It will all work out, you mark my words. Listen, you know I'm right." I can't say that I shared his total confidence. However, I hoped that he would prove to be right. I left the shop to find that it was raining heavily. It was fine earlier so I was not wearing a topcoat. I made my way past lots of scurrying people hurrying out of the rain. Once I was over the bridge and onto the towpath, I saw puddles everywhere with ripples appearing on the surface of the canal. The sound of it was like a roar and, by this time, I was absolutely drenched. Once alone, I touched my specs and set the display.

In seconds, I was back outside my apartment. To my amazement it was a fine day. The sun was shining, making my wet clothes steam. Several people were in the foyer looking at me and then outside, chattering amongst themselves. But at that moment, I can honestly say I just didn't care what they were thinking about me. Going into the bathroom, I took off my wet clothes — everything was clinging to my skin. Thinking on it now, I must have been a sorry spectacle in the foyer. Taking a towel, I wiped my face and looked in the mirror. My face was very flushed, maybe from embarrassment. Taking a good long shower, I finally emerged feeling at least a bit refreshed. What a day it had turned out to be. I thought to myself, *Just how many more things can go wrong?* I dressed, and then rustled up some food and drink for myself. I had long since got into the habit of eating and drinking on a regular basis, not wishing to repeat some of my early mistakes.

Now, feeling better, I sat in the lounge and began to go through the logistics for my trips to replenish my stock. These trips would need a lot of finance so I would also have to include some more visits to the bookmakers — omitting Mr Rossi's place of course. I didn't want to cause any more problems. Once ready I made my final preparations for my trips. I was hoping that this would be my biggest and most successful foray into the past so far.

Chapter 15

Albums Galore

I decided that my first port of call must be to the bookmakers. Armed with my notepad containing lots of race results, I made my way to 'Worthington's Bookmakers' on Phelam Street. I had now become much more cautious with my betting than in the beginning—now purposely losing more than previously, to appear more realistic. However, today I needed some good wins. Reaching the shop, I went in and placed my bets. I opened the door when suddenly I received the shock of my life when I was met by someone pushing me right back into the shop. A voice loomed out saying, "Well, well, if it isn't, Jack, or whatever your name is." Then he shouted, "Can we go in the back, Bill?" Going into the back room, I was thrust onto a chair. In the room was Bill Worthington, the owner of the premises, and of course a certain Mr Rossi. Dave had his hands on my shoulders, with his feet astride my legs. Staring very closely into my eyes he said, "What are we to do with you?"

"What do you mean exactly?" I responded.

Mint Vinyl

"Don't get cocky with me, sunshine. Did you hear that, Bill? He doesn't know what we're on about.

Bill said, "If you believe that, you'll believe anything."

"Exactly. Is he still winning his bets, Bill?" Asked Rossi.

"Not every bet, but he still wins too many for my liking!"

Then Rossi said, "Now you listen here, pal, your betting round here stops now. Do you hear me—it stops!" I could see that Dave was at the end of his tether, his face red and snarling.

I foolishly said, "Okay, 'Dave,' I'll do just what you say."

Grabbing hold of my shirt, he lifted me upright in front of his face and snorted, "Mr Rossi to you. Friends call me Dave, and you, pal, are no friend of mine—or anybody else round here for that matter." Pushing me back down into the chair, he said, "Anyway, we have a treat in store for you. And you can go now!" I just got up and started to make my may out when Dave shouted after me, "One more thing, Jack, or whatever or whoever you are. Don't bother trying to collect your winnings because they didn't win, okay!"

Leaving the shop, I was shaking visibly, but glad to be in one piece. Dave was really pent up in there—it could have been much worse—remembering my encounter with a certain Mr Wilson. Sure enough, Dave was really angry, it was about more than that I thought. Suddenly, as I walked along, a wry smile came to my face. When I think about it, our Mr Rossi never seemed to believe a single word that I said to him—not even my name. I couldn't for the life of me think why. *Anyway, back to reality,* I thought. I now needed some ready cash. I had savings, but I had big plans for those. So, it was off to a bookmakers further afield. After an excellent day at the races so to speak.

I then went to see Tony with some of my orders. Tony said to me, "Nice to see you after such a long time." I was taken aback for a second and then realised that from Tony's perspective it had indeed been quite a long time. I then returned home with lots of albums. After that it was back again to other years — I was to and fro all day long. Tony and Lucy seemed fine with things, but we didn't really talk about much other than fulfilling my orders. I couldn't help seeing some changes in myself. I was missing seeing April very much, but in a way, it had helped because it would have been much sadder to have seen her. Over the next few days, I made repeated trips to Tony's.

Soon enough, I had enough stock to afford myself a well-earned break. I spent a few days back at home just trying to relax. The beauty of the time device was that I could return just when I wanted to. After resting and restocking the shops, I made a call to Phillipa. She was delighted to hear from me. I told her that I had given much thought to her business proposition, adding that I would love to see her again. She told me that she would call into the shop that day, to which I replied, "I look forward to it."

As I walked to the shop of Clifton Road, my mind was working overtime with all that was going on in my two

Mint Vinyl

lives. I arrived early so that I could have the distraction of meeting people who called into the shop. I got talking to this one guy called Robert. He had come to pick up the Stones' first album from sixty-four. It was just so good to see his eyes light up as I handed it to him. This was what it was all about for me. We talked about the tracks—he loved *Route 66*, *Tell me*, and *Mona*. This guy was so pleased he walked around the shop just holding up his prize! All too soon, the exhilaration of all this had to end. It would soon be time for Phillipa to arrive.

She duly entered the shop, looking stunning once again. We went into the stock room come office. She said she had another meeting to attend, so we got right down to it. She began saying, "What I'm proposing, Jack, is that I redesign the website and look after all the orders generated from it. Also, I would like to invest in the company if that would be acceptable."

"Absolutely," I said, "that sounds excellent." We would discuss the finances in more detain when we met again.

"So sorry it has to be short and sweet," she said, "just so much happening at the moment. I will get on with the website right away and I'll be in touch. Speak soon!"

"Okay, that's brilliant. Look forward to it, take care." As quickly as she came, she was gone like a whirlwind. I was more than pleased with the outcome of our somewhat brief encounter.

Albums Galore

I spent some more time in the shop, after which I returned home for lunch. I changed afterwards to return to the sixties. I set my displays to arrive a couple of days after my last visit to sixty-three. I got to Tony's, finding him seeming quite pleased. The council had agreed to a meeting. I told Tony, "I'm there for you, Tony, anytime, my friend."

Tony replied, "Listen, I'm lucky to have a friend like you." I couldn't help but think to myself, *Not half as much as I am to have a friend like Tony – he doesn't know the half of it.* I decided to write a note and post it through April's door. It read:

> *I miss you so very much April my sweetheart. I just wanted you to know that I am respecting your wish for some time and space, but it's difficult not seeing you.*
>
> *All my love,*
>
> *Jack*

I called back into Tony's, picking up a few albums he had got for me from the States. I left, saying that I would see them soon. Tony said, "Come for tea on Friday."

Lucy said, "Yeah, that will be fab, Uncle Jack. I would like a good natter to you, haven't talked much lately."

"It's a date then," I said, "I'll be here. Get your favourite songs ready to play."

Mint Vinyl

On returning home I found a card behind my door from DC Robert Fuller, asking me to contact him on the number written on the card. After making myself a coffee, I go the phone and called him. "Hi, DC Fuller, Jack Roberts here. You asked me to contact you."

"Ah yes, Mr Roberts. I wonder if you could call round to the station today. I need to ask a few more questions about your business."

"Okay, when do you need me?"

"Would 2pm be alright with you?"

"Yes, that will be fine."

"Just ask for me at the desk and we'll take it from there."

After the call, the first thing to come into my mind was Phillip Johnson—*I'll guarantee he's behind all this*, I though. Just the thought of him was enough to get me agitated. I sat back and tried to think about the situation, but my mind seemed to be a jumble of so many things. More searching questions about the business was about the last thing I needed right then.

Soon enough, it was time to make my way to the station and, having changed, I made my way there. On arriving I asked at the desk. Sergeant Wilde said, "Go into the office. DC Fuller is expecting you." I knocked on the door.

"Come in," said DC Fuller. I entered and DC Fuller stood to greet me, holding his hand out to shake mine. Having received a firm handshake, DC Fuller said, "Please take a seat."

Albums Galore

Before he had a chance to speak, I said, "This is the work of Phillip Johnson, isn't it?"

"I'm not at liberty to discuss details like that, Mr Roberts. I just need some information regarding your suppliers."

"Well, I did tell you some at our last meeting."

"That turned out to be a bit of a dead end I'm afraid. So, if you could be a little more specific, I would be very appreciative."

"The thing is... my supplier wishes to remain anonymous. Surely you can appreciate that, DC Fuller."

"I understand that, but I must admit that even I myself am intrigued as to how you come to acquire these mint condition albums."

"I can see your point of view, but even if I could tell you, believe me, you just wouldn't believe what I had to say!"

"Are you sure that you have nothing further that you can say on this matter?"

"Nothing else. What now?"

"All I can say at the moment, Mr Roberts, is I will have to inform my superiors and we'll take it from there." Shaking my hand again, he said, "We'll be in touch."

Leaving the police station, my thoughts were very much focused on the present events. I had no idea where this was leading. Even if I told the whole truth, it would make no difference. *Maybe it will have to come to that*, I thought. Life just seemed so complicated at that moment. Who would have thought that putting a smile on people's faces could

Mint Vinyl

bring about so much hardship? At home, I made an early dinner as I was feeling quite peckish. After eating, I sat down and tried to relax. Despite all the problems I needed to stay strong, this was not simply about me.

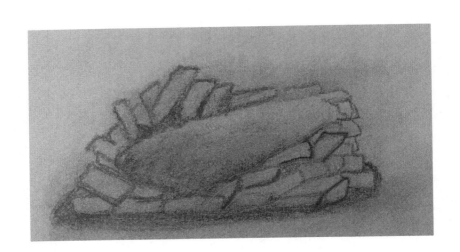

Chapter 16

Tony's Good News

Returning to Tony's in sixty-three, I was so pleased to find out that Tony had heard via the grapevine, that his licence application was likely to be approved by the council. The day of the meeting arrived, and I arrived at Tony's in good time. Once ready, we made our way to the council offices in Tony's car. Once in, as predicted, and as I had deduced from my visits to Tony in the future — well from that point in time anyway — all things went well. Tony and I emerged with the licence. Tony was visibly relieved about the whole thing — it had really been getting him down. We went back to the shop. Tony went in first, holding the licence in the air and punching the air with his other hand. Lucy was delighted, letting out a nervous laugh. It was so good to see then happy again.

Tony said, "Listen, Janette will be over the moon when she gets home from work." Tony put his arm around my shoulder and said, "Listen, Jack, I know we said Friday for tea, but I feel like celebrating tonight. What do you say?"

Mint Vinyl

I was speechless for a moment, then I just said, "Absolutely."

"Great. When Janette arrives home, we will go out for a meal—the three of us." No sooner than Tony had spoken those words, the whole thing for me was tinged with sadness—normally it would have been the four of us. All my thoughts turned to April and our difficulties. The meal was a fish and chip meal, but it was like old times. Getting back to Tony's I said to everyone, "Let's round off the evening watching some music videos on my tablet." After this I made my way back to my apartment and went to bed.

Having just showered and eaten breakfast, I was relaxing reading the local paper, when, to my great surprise, my doorbell rang—no-one ever called at this time. Opening the door, I was amazed to find Phillipa holding a pint of milk from my front door, saying, "Morning, Jack, you're looking very casual." This was probably due to the fact that I was still in my pyjamas and dressing gown.

"Forgive my appearance," I said.

"Nonsense, I like to see real people."

"Come in and take a seat. Would you like a coffee? I've got some on."

"I'd love one, thanks. Cream and one sugar for me please."

I brought the coffee and said, "I will just be a few moments while I dress."

Tony's Good News

"Okay, that's fine, I have a free day today." Once dressed I returned to the lounge to join Phillipa.

"Have you taken breakfast yet?" I asked.

"No, not as yet. How about we go to a local café, then we can talk." Unfortunately, I had already eaten, but at a pinch I could manage a bacon barm or something.

We found a nice café and took breakfast together — then we talked.

"Firstly, about business," Phillipa said, "I would like to have a stake in this crazy business."

I replied, "How do you mean crazy?"

"Well, all these mint condition albums, where do you get them from, Jack?" My mind jerked into action — yet another inquisitive mind, *Just what I need*, I thought. Then she said, "Look, Jack, I have been so pleased to meet up with you again, and I must say that I really like you. Don't get me wrong, as a friend I mean, not romantically." Well at least that was a relief. "I would like us to become very good friends, Jack, I would like that a lot. What do you say, Mr Roberts?"

"Honestly, I would love that. You're such an amazing woman — who wouldn't want you as a friend?"

"Good, that's settled then. No pressure, in your own time, Jack, when you feel you can open up to me, I'm a good listener. I hope that you will see that you can trust me implicitly."

Mint Vinyl

We spent the next few hours driving in the countryside in my car. We spent a lovely day together. She really was a smart and very charming businesswoman—no wonder she was doing so well for herself. Already, I found myself admiring her greatly.

Over the next couple of weeks, things on the whole were pretty quiet. There had been no word from the police in my time, and, although the posse still hung around Tony's sometimes, there had been no real visits from Mr Rossi himself. I couldn't help but think that it was the calm before the storm. On the business front, things could not have been better. Phillipa's revamp of the website was really paying dividends—the orders had shot up and I was very impressed. We had spoken on the phone lots but hadn't met face to face for a while as we were both extremely busy.

I had been looking forward to spending time again with Tony in his workshop. Now that we were legal, he wanted to work on the backlog of repairs. On arriving at Tony's, Lucy as ever was very pleased to see me. She gave me a big smile and hug, saying, "Uncle Jack, it's always so good to see you. Thanks for helping dad."

"I love to spend time with you all—you are family."

"Go on through, Uncle Jack, Dad is already in there."

"Okay, see you in a while."

Tony got up from his bench to shake my hand, saying, "Listen, like old times eh."

"Sure is good to be back," I replied.

Tony's Good News

Before we started work on some of the repairs Tony told me that April had left something for me. I had received word back from my note to April, in the form of a note—she wanted me to call round to her place that evening. After telling Tony the contents of the note, he said, "Listen, I know it's been hard for you not seeing April, but she's a good kid you know, and this whole two-lives thing, it's hard to get your head round it yer know."

"I can see that you have questions, Tony, and I'll be happy to try to answer them. You know how I feel about you all."

"It's just such a huge thing, yer know what I mean. For instance, you don't say all that much about your other life do you, Jack?"

"That's not because I'm being evasive. I feel that you have enough on your plate right here. I don't believe that you need to hear my problems as well."

"Listen, Jack mate, I'm not being nosy or anything, more inquisitive about things. You don't go into any detail about things in your time."

"Okay, what would you like to know." I must have had a very serious face because Tony just burst into laughter.

"You're face, Jack, it's a picture. I'm just interested, I don't' want to grill you."

"Okay, okay, maybe I'm a bit too serious sometimes."

"Listen, I was just trying to get a picture of how times have changed. After all, here where I live is where you live

177

more or less." I gave Tony some insight into life in the 21st century — he seemed quite puzzled with it all. Suddenly remembering that I had my mobile phone in my pocket, I took it out and placed it on the bench.

"What do you make of that?" I asked.

He picked it up and gave it a close inspection, then said, "You got me, what is it?"

"It's a phone."

"A phone. How can that be a phone?"

"Well, it's a mobile phone." I then explained about satellites and masts and things — I think it was all too much at once for Tony. Then I said to him, "This is the funniest thing for me — back in my time, people let this small electronic device rule their lives. You would be amazed to see it, believe me." Now it was my turn for laughter.

"Listen, how would you let that happen?"

"Tony, that's exactly why I'm laughing."

"Seems like a very strange world to me, Jack."

"Oh, it is alright, trust me."

Chapter 17

Meeting April

Leaving Tony's, I made my way to April's place. She welcomed me in, and we both started to talk. I apologised saying, "You speak first."

She said, "Well you know that I've been finding it difficult that you have two lives. I have given it a lot of thought and I just have some questions for you."

"Fire away," I said, "whatever you need to ask."

"Is there someone that you're fond of?"

"There is only my mum, and I don't see her very much. So no, there isn't. I take it you mean is there a woman in my life. Only you April — only you."

"It's just that we have spoken so little about your life in the future, and even though I seem to have just gone along with everything, that's simply down to the fact of falling in love with you, Jack."

"That's all my fault. It's a bad failing on my part. I simply don't share things as readily as I should. I'm much too private. From now on I will promise to be much more open and transparent."

Mint Vinyl

"My dear Jack, sometimes just the way you put things lightens my mood. I find the way you speak rather amusing. You are from Dansford, yet you speak so different."

"That will be down to being raised by my auntie and uncle. They were very well educated and well-spoken. April, does this mean that our relationship is back on again?"

"Yes, Jack, back on for good I hope." That settled, I headed back to Tony's to share my good news.

Back at my apartment, I began to mull over the events of the day. I decided that I must be much more open — with the people who matter to me that is. There was a lot of logistical stuff to go through, so I made a start. Once again, there were some very nasty remarks concerning myself and the business. I suspected that these were all from you know who, although I couldn't prove that it was from him as each comment came from a different username. Also checking my phone, I found some messages from Phillipa and one from Angela, the latter saying that we had some notes posted through the letter box, and that she needed to see my ASAP. After sorting out my logistics, I visited the shop. Speaking with Angela, she handed me a couple of notes. Each note was an A4 sheet with words cut from a newspaper or something. The first read:

BEWARE ABOUT WHAT YOU ARE DOING

WE LIKE IT NOT

Meeting April

I thought it a rather strange term. The second one began in a similar vein, but went on to say:

IF YOU CARRY ON

THERE WILL BE A PRICE TO PAY

I thought to myself, *More handiwork of our Mr Johnson.* I spoke to all my staff to apologise for them having to deal with such things. I told them that if there were any more, they should just put them right into the bin — which is where these two notes were headed. In some ways I could understand him being aggrieved, but this was not the way to go about it. After spending some time in the shop, I was feeling much better about things. The shop was such a joy, and my staff were just brilliant It was like a well-oiled machine. Checking the messages from Phillipa, I saw that she wanted to meet with me again, so I gave her a call. I said, "Phillipa, hi, it's Jack. I wonder if you would like to eat in at my place tonight."

"That sounds great," she said, "is 7:30 okay?"

"Ok, it's a date. Well, not a date — you know what I mean." There was laughter on the other end and a bright red face on me. I just found her somewhat unnerving — I guess it was just me.

Chapter 18

Opening Up

7:30pm arrived and so did Phillipa, right on time. The doorbell rang, and I answered, greeted by a warm smile. She said in her characteristic whisper of a voice, "Nice to see you, Jack."

"Come in, let me take your coat." After a takeaway Indian and a couple of glasses of wine, we got talking. She pulled no punches and put me firmly on the spot.

She said, "Tell me truthfully, Jack, where do you source your records? Come now, Jack, you know me by now — I have your best interests at heart" Since being reunited, so to speak, with Phillipa, I had seen her integrity shine through everything she did.

"I do trust you, my dear Phillipa, that's why I would first of all ask your advice on a small but delicate matter."

"You have me intrigued now," she said. I proceeded to relate to her everything concerning Phillip Johnson, to which she replied, "That's just awful, Jack. He doesn't seem a very nice man." She then went on to make a very valid point about the whole situation. What she said kind of

Mint Vinyl

stopped me in my tracks. For the first time in months, I saw that my overwhelming desire to fulfil my dreams had completely clouded my senses. By this I mean that I never stopped to consider the consequences of providing mint condition albums on a large scale. Only now did I start to realise all the ramifications that my actions might have. Phillipa said, "I in no way condone this man's actions, but he has got a somewhat legitimate grievance don't you think, Jack?" And therein lay the trouble—I hadn't been thinking. As a result of our conversation, I also told her about the police being involved.

With my head in my hands, and Phillipa's hand round my shoulder, I said, "What can I do, Phillipa, just what can I do? It's a total mess."

She said, "Jack my love, try to get some sleep. I'm going home now. I will ring you in the morning and we will get this whole thing sorted."

"Okay, I will try." At first, I slept for about four hours— I was just exhausted. Then, afterwards, I was wide awake thinking about all of this. This wasn't my dream—this was more of a nightmare.

It was now the early morning, and I was sitting in my lounge in the dark. My heart was racing, and my mind was on fire. I asked myself over and over again, just how had it gotten to this? After dozing for a while, I awoke to daylight streaming though my window, my blinds still open from yesterday. I now needed to pull myself together. My phone

Opening Up

rang—it was Phillipa. She asked how I was feeling, to which I lied saying, "Okay." She told me that she would come over to the shop for 9:30am. "I'll be there," I said, "and, Phillipa, thanks for last night for…"

She interrupted saying, "It was nothing, see you soon."

I arrived at the shop, trying to be positive for my staff, but my mind was elsewhere. Phillipa arrived and we went into the back. I had decided that she deserved to know the whole truth—I would tell her everything, the whole shooting match. I needed—no, not just needed—desperately needed someone to know everything in the present time.

Chapter 19

Amazement

As she began to speak, I somewhat rudely interrupted saying, "Phillipa, there are some things that I must tell you!" From my behaviour she could see that I was, shall I say, rather agitated. She was now for her part looking quite worried.

"What is it, Jack, that's got you in this state?" she asked. I started from the very beginning, telling her about my father's accident on a motorbike when I was very young. How he was hospitalised for two years, then spent the rest of his life in a wheelchair, and how my mum had suffered a breakdown as a result. I explained that because of these events I had been raised by Uncle George and Auntie Suzanne, telling Phillipa that they had influenced my whole life. I then went on to tell her of my uncle's work for the RAF and what he had done for me to secure my dreams. To say that she was amazed is an understatement. Dumbfounded would, I think, be a better term.

"So, Phillipa, there you have it. Now you know everything, and your questions regarding how I acquire my stock are now answered. It's rather simple when you are able to travel in time." She seemed to be dealing with my revelations rather well, when suddenly the phone rang—it was the police.

Phillipa said, "Answer it, Jack." She hung around until after the call—after which I filled her in on what DC Fuller had to say. "You go along and just play it by ear," she said, "see what he has to say before you are forthcoming." She then confessed to being somewhat stunned by what I had relayed to her, and that she needed time to think, but added, "Don't worry, Jack, we can work all these things out."

DC Fuller wanted me to call to the station at 11:30am that morning. He had told me that there had been some further developments. Once again, my mind was thrown into a quandary—my life seemed to lurch from one problem to the next.

When I arrived, Sergeant Wilde was on the desk. He motioned for me to go on through, so I knocked on the door and entered. I was greeted once more by Fuller's firm but warm handshake. I must confess that I didn't dislike him at all, he was very polite and well-mannered—in different circumstances I believe we could have even been friends.

After taking a seat he said, "Well, Mr Roberts, I contacted my superiors and they agreed to let me put into action a plan that I had formulated. Namely, that one of our young PCs would purchase an album from your shop. He reported as to having a very good conversation with you, sir. His

Amazement

name is PC Robert Jones. As part of the plan, he purchased a 'Rolling Stones' album I believe. He was very pleased with his purchase and extends his thanks. However, the purchase was a vital element in our inquiries. We passed it on to a group of experts to examine. That's why it has taken a few weeks. They reported back with the news that the album is indeed genuine. You see, Mr Roberts, our real concern was that there may have been an operation in place manufacturing copies of original recordings, in breach of copyright law, and therefore a very serious crime."

What he had said literally took my breath away. Phillipa had been right in what she had said to me. In my utter exuberance I had not engaged my brain at all — none of these implications had even remotely crossed my mind. What a complete fool I had been.

Then, to my complete surprise, he said, "So that's it as far as we are concerned, Mr Roberts. No crime has been committed, so you can go."

I said, "So you don't' need to know my suppliers then."

"No sir, we don't. The articles in question are authentic so that's that."

I said, "On a personal level, I would like to reveal how I acquire my stock." He looked rather puzzled. "My business associate assures me that honesty is always the best policy." I related to him how I was able to travel back in time.

He looked at me straight in the eyes and said, "Mr Roberts, you are an intelligent man, and I can't think why you would want to concoct such a story as that, but you and I both know that that's not possible. So, we'll leave it at that, just between you and me." Rising from his seat, he extended his hand to shake mine saying, "Goodbye, Mr Roberts, look after yourself."

To which I replied, "And also to you, DC Fuller." Well, at least I had been honest, but just as I had expected, no one would ever believe me — well that wasn't quite true. There were some that did, but they were mostly from another time, there was only Phillipa in my own time.

As I made my way home, I decided to call Phillipa. As soon as I got in, I called her.

I said, "Hi, it's Jack."

Immediately she said, "How did things go with the police?"

"Very well actually, very well indeed."

"I'm just about to meet with a client."

"Ok, I mustn't keep you, give me a call."

"I'll do that and arrange a meeting. I still have lots of questions for you, Jack."

I changed and made preparations to go and see Tony. I was also hoping to spend some time with April — things had improved on that front, and I wanted things to continue in that vein so that we could have our wonderful relationship back again. I saw Lucy and Tony first. They both seemed very chirpy, and all seemed well. However, I was a little

Amazement

concerned about some of my visits into the future. They had both seemed very pre-occupied about something.

I asked Tony directly, "Has there been any developments then, Tony?"

He looked at me puzzled and said, "No, nothing at all. It's been very quiet on the Rossi front if that's what you mean." That was exactly what I meant. Then I was suddenly struck with a thought. Here I was in 1963, when some of these things appeared to be happening in 1965. All this time travel even had me confused sometimes. Tony and I went into the workshop to do some repairs. Tony was getting much more work now and was really appreciative of my help. As we were working, Tony suddenly spun around on his stool. Looking straight at me he said, "Listen, Jack, I'm curious. I know that I've never pushed you on this, but I would love to know more about you — personally I mean."

I replied, "I know, I'm not exactly an open book, but I will try and answer any questions."

"You say that you are from round here, from Dansford I mean."

"Yes I am."

"It's just, well, you don't exactly talk the way we do, Jack, if you know what I mean."

I gave a little chuckle and said, "That's probably my upbringing." I then related to him about how my Uncle George and Auntie Suzanne were as some might think, quite posh. However, even though my uncle was rather eccentric, he

Mint Vinyl

was not stand-offish with anyone. Thinking this way, a picture appeared in my mind of my uncle in his suit and tie, with his thick bushy hair, big moustache, and sideburns. Even on the hottest of days, that would be my uncle's attire. He would always say, "There's never any excuse for not looking your best."

Tony said, "You speak of them with great affection. They must have meant so much to you."

"Yes, I was so fortunate to be raised by them." We also talked about my parents and how things had worked out. I was glad to share something with Tony — he was a very good listener. And, above that, it felt good to be sharing things. I had always seemed to keep things so much to myself.

Then Tony lightened the mood — smiling he said, "So, how old then, Jack? I have you down for being forty."

"You're just too kind," I replied, "add another eight and you're there."

"Well, you do surprise me, you're looking good I must say."

I laughed and said, "Let's get on with these repairs." When it was after six, I said to Tony that I was going over to April's.

Tony said, "Listen, give her my love, Jack. So glad things are better again for you two."

Getting to April's, she let me in and said, "Take a seat, I've got the tea on." We ate and spent a nice evening to-

Amazement

gether. She still had lots of questions about my life, but we were once again good, and I was so happy about that. April was such a wonderful, unexpected part of my life. A wave of contentment passed over me, and I savoured this rare moment of ease.

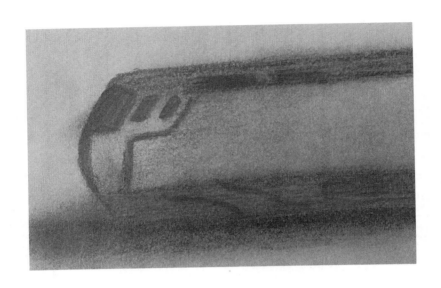

Chapter 20

The Seventies

I was now enjoying a time when things seemed a lot more settled in the present time—apart from Mr Johnson still being something of a nuisance now and again. On the whole, things were much better, notwithstanding the fact that I could now confide in Phillipa about every part of business. In the early sixties, Tony was having some respite from Mr Rossi and his posse. All this tranquillity led me to think that I could put into action a planned trip to the seventies—1973 to be precise. A number of things had brought this about. I had received many orders for both albums and singles from this time period, and there were a number of artists that I wanted the opportunity to see live. So, for these reasons, my destination would be the city of Manchester. I planned to first travel to Dansford and then to Manchester by train, staying there for four days. I had put in a lot of time into planning this trip, with the logistics of acquiring records, the location of record shops, where each artist will appear, and, as I intended to make this a very lucrative trip, the location of several bookmakers far from Mr Rossi's influence.

Mint Vinyl

There was one last thing that I intended to do while in town. I planned to visit a jewellers to purchase an engagement ring for April. I wanted to surprise her after my trip — or before in one sense. I had — at least I hoped — been meticulous in my planning. Checking over the details once more, I began to feel quite exhausted. I intended to get a good night's sleep, so I retired to bed with, for the first time in what seemed like an age, happy thoughts.

I got a very good sleep; my alarm woke me at 6am. I had a very good feeling about my upcoming trip. I packed a bag and changed into casual wear after a good shower. After breakfast, I made all the preparations for my trip. I turned on the radio, got my specs from the drawer, and set the displays for '73. Feeling a little nervous, I thought to myself, *There is a lot riding on this trip*. A smile came to my face with this thought, as I would be going to various bookmakers — the funny side of this was not lost on me.

My train was to leave for Manchester from Dansford station at 9:30am. I needed to buy a ticket when I arrived — no advance bookings online in this era. I had brought with me a large suitcase for my purchases, as well as a bag containing my clothes. I had set the time for 8:30am to reach the station without rushing. Once on the towpath I immediately saw changes. New lighting had appeared on this section of the canal leading to the bridge and the locks. The old lock keeper's cottage had now gone completely, while it had just been in ruin in the early sixties. Everywhere

The Seventies

seemed brighter and much cleaner. I noticed from the large board displaying the business residing in the old mill, that some had changed. The company making gardening equipment had been replaced with a window company called 'Paynes for Windows' — a slight play on words. There was also an electrical wholesale company operating there called 'Travis Electrics.' Even though it was relatively early in the morning, there were a good number of people on the towpath. Many people had very different hairstyles than in the sixties — a lot of longer hair, and that was only the men. I was also reminded of Uncle George, as many of these men were sporting long bushy sideburns and moustaches. I must say that I was already liking the seventies very much. Lots of people exchanged good mornings with me. One man, looking at my suitcase, shouted to me, "Off on holiday, chief, or doing some more filming?" I looked at him puzzled. He pointed at my suitcase and said, "Man in a suitcase, squire," then walked away shaking his head and chuckling away to himself.

I made my way to a taxi office to get a taxi to Dansford station. The driver was called Frank, a chatty guy, very friendly. He also asked if I was going on holiday, "Gettin' away from it all eh, pal. I don't blame yer, gets yer down round 'ere sometimes."

I said, "It's not really a holiday as such, more of a business trip."

"What game are you in then, pal?"

Mint Vinyl

"The record business, I have two shops." A thought flashed through my mind about what I had just said, and I quickly added that the shops were in Brenton.

Frank started laughing, saying, "Blimey, chief, I weren't gonna put the thumbscrews on yer." My answer must have seemed very abrupt. I thought to myself, *I must be more careful in my conversations*. Frank had a family picture in his cab, so I engaged him with that—he thought the world of his wife and family. We reached the station, and I gave him a tip to which he said, "Cheers, chief, have a good trip." Off he went in a shot.

I was now standing outside the station with my suitcase and bag in hand. A wave of excitement flooded through me—I was really looking forward to staying in Manchester. I walked in and found the ticket office and bought my ticket. I had 25 minutes before my train. Going to the station buffet, I ordered a tea and a scone with jam. The scone was passable, but the tea was awful. After taking one mouthful I remembered what my mum always said about it—one word, 'Stewed'. I would have liked to spit it out, but that was not exactly the done thing. Going to my platform, I showed my ticket, got it clipped, and, finding a carriage, I got in. I thought to myself, *Wow, this is fantastic, so much more atmospheric than train journeys in my time.* I shared the compartment with a young, recently married couple from Dansford—Josie and Bill Prentice. After our introductions, we got into conversations about this and that and the other, just general chit chat really. Then Bill said, "So what line of work are you in then, Jack?"

I replied, but making sure I came across normally this time, "I'm in the record business. I have two shops in Brenton." This last part was of course an out and out lie, but this time travel business brought about some things that didn't sit well with me, no not at all. I tried to console myself that they were necessary, but I still didn't like having to tell lies. I asked Bill, "So tell me, Bill, what do you do for a living?"

He replied, "We both work for the railways. After getting married we decided on a fresh start. We applied for jobs in Manchester, and we got them, so we're on an adventure. New beginnings so to speak." They added that they would rent somewhere to live while they got on their feet. I was very impressed by their obvious enthusiasm and with their love for each other. This prompted thoughts of my lovely April. When we arrived in Manchester I wished them all the best, adding that I was sure that they would have a great life together.

Now, standing alone on the platform—well not really alone—I paused momentarily. A drove of passengers from my train then jostled by me. There were people shouting, laughing, and lots of talking. Many people were coming onto the platform to meet with loved ones. It was a veritable sea of humanity. Eventually I got down to the gate where a ticket collector looked at my ticket. "Return," he duly punched it saying, "Good morning to you, sir." I walked out into the station concourse. The scene that was before me had me quite dumbfounded. I believed there to be a lot of people on the platform, well that was nothing compared with this. The hustle and bustle of people about their business was absolutely fascinating. There were many people queuing at the ticket offices, droves of people thronging around the various kiosks, and every now and then the thunderous echoing voice of the station announcer was heard, but try as I might, I could make out very little of what he said. Lots of travellers were grouped around the large boards, seeking information on their respective trains. I just stood for a few moments taking it all in. *This is wonderful*, I thought to myself. What a contrast between this and the start my journey at the small station in Dansford. Looking for the signs for the way out, I made my way to the exit.

Once outside I was greeted by a light drizzle, the kind that soaks you through in no time at all. There were taxis waiting outside the station, so I spoke to one of the drivers, asking if he knew any local B&Bs not too far away. He said, "Hop in, chief, out of the rain. I'll get your luggage." The driver got back in saying, "The name's Bill, Bill gates. Nice to meet you."

I swallowed hard, and replied, "Jack Roberts."

"An old mate of mine has just come back into town to help his mum with the B&B. Len Docman, good bloke Len. He'll sort you out, squire.

The Seventies

"Okay, that sounds great, Bill." As we drove along, I observed lot of people toing and froing, women with umbrellas, men walking along with upturned collars, and some people sheltering in doorways. In what seemed like no time at all, we arrived at 'The Majestic Bed & Breakfast', run by Mrs Irene Docman and her son Len. I paid my fare and Bill drove off. Before I walked to the front door I had a little chuckle to myself, thinking, *It's not every day that Bill Gates drives you in his taxi.*

Ringing the bell, I stood and waited for a moment. A man, who I presumed to be Len, opened the door. "Come in out of the rain pal," he said.

"Thank you," I replied. We entered the hallway, nice and bright, well decorated, with a wooden floor.

"Just put your things there a mo. I'll sort them in a minute. Len's the name, Len Docman. And you are?"

"Jack Roberts."

"Nice to meet yer, Jack. Just follow me to reception." We walked through to reception and met Mrs Docman, a petite lady, smartly dressed, grey hair, and a lovely smile. "Mum, this is Jack Roberts. Jack, this is my mum Irene."

"A pleasure to meet you Mrs Docman," I said.

"Likewise," she replied. I extended my hand to her. She responded and I clasped her hand between mine. I smiled at her, and she said, "Well, now that's a charmer for sure, Jack."

"How long will you be stayin', Jack?" said Len.

Mint Vinyl

"Four days for now," I answered, "but we'll see how it goes." Len got me the key to room four and said, "Follow me, I'll show you to yer room. I'll bring yer bags in a mo." The room was excellent—neutral colours, high ceilings, comfortable bed, with an ensuite bathroom. *This will do very nicely*, I thought. A few minutes later, Len brought up my bags saying, "Get yerself settled then come down and join us for a brew. Like strong tea der yer, Jack?"

"Yes, I do thank you." I put my suitcase and bag onto the bed and stood at the window. Looking out I could see a good number of people hurrying backwards and forwards along Cheetham Street. I couldn't help but wonder where they were all going, each one with their own lives.

Later on, I went down to meet Irene and Len for a cup of tea. We chatted for a while, telling them that it was Bill Gates who recommended them to me. They laughed and Len said, "Great guy Bill. What a character. He's always banging on about these little machines changing people's lives in the future. Computers he calls them, I ask you!"

At this I was lost for words—I just said, "Fancy that." I took my leave of them, saying that I was sorting out my clothes and things. That being done, I looked out of the window once more. There were now lots more people about now. The day had finally brightened up. I went and told Len, "I'm off out for a walk."

"Okay, Jack, take this key with you, later tonight I'll be going to 'The Feathers' if you fancy a pint."

The Seventies

"See you later for that," I replied.

I decided that it would be good to do some searching around for some record shops and for some bookmakers. I had lots of race results with me in my notebook. I had not walked far before coming across a betting shop. The sign read, 'John Fredericks Turf Accountant'. The shop was large, but nicer than a certain Mr Rossi's place, and I was surprised to find young women behind the counter as well as men. I got a slip and placed a bet with only fifteen minutes before the race, so I didn't have long to wait. Soon I was collecting my winnings. As I got another slip and began to write it out, a guy came up to me and said, "Sid's the name, pal. Couldn't help but notice your good win. Don't suppose you could give me a hot tip? Not been going well lately."

"Why not," I said. *Can't do any harm*, I thought to myself. I wrote on the slip for him saying, "There you go, Sid, put what you want on it. It's a winner. He was very happy when his horse romped home.

He collected his winnings smiling from ear to ear, but not without saying, "Thanks pal, thanks a bundle." I didn't intend to make it a habit, but I did get a warm glow inside. After some more wins and losses — more wins than losses, but you can't be too careful — I walked around and found a couple of good record shops. The shops were very well stocked and would serve me very well in purchasing the stock that I required. However, at this point I was only browsing. Tomorrow would be the real deal.

It was now getting later in the afternoon. Spotting a fish-chip bar, I decided to go in. Got to say that the food was excellent, as well as the service. I dined in and was well looked after by a charming waitress called Maureen. Feeling much the better for my repast, I left after settling my bill and saying thanks. Walking round for a little while longer, I came across some more bookmakers and another record shop. *This is going to be a very profitable trip*, I thought.

As I let myself in, Len was at the reception and said, "Good day, Jack? Weather picked up a bit for yer? Did yer enjoy your walk?"

"Yes thanks." I replied.

"Still on for 'The Feathers' later, Jack?"

"Definitely. What time will you be leaving?"

"About 7:30."

"Okay, see you then." I went up to my room, deciding to try and have a nap—it had been a long day. I must have dozed off for about an hour, waking just after 7pm. I went down for half past, Len meeting me in the hallway.

"Right then, off we go," he said. 'The Feathers' was about ten minutes' walk away, so we were soon there. As with the sixties, the pub was very smoky and noisy, but on the plus side was nicely decorated and was a large premises. I was surprised to see many young people in there, and I commented to Len about it. "It's the live music. The kids love

The Seventies

it." Len told me that it was a local band tonight, a five-piece outfit called The Throws. Len ordered two pints and we found a table. "So, what brings you to Manchester then, Jack?" he asked.

"Business and pleasure," I said.

"What business is that then? If you don't mind me askin'."

"I own two record shops in Dansford, so I'm here to check out the shops. Always on the lookout for stock."

"And the pleasure?"

"I want to catch some live bands whilst I'm here. How's about you, Len, what's your story?"

"Builder by trade, got a job in York — project manager on a big site — but came back home six months ago. Dad died just over twelve months ago. Thought Mum was okay after the funeral but she weren't doing too good at all. The place was being neglected, so I came back. Don't want to see the old place fail." We chatted some more, and I got us another pint. Soon it was time for the group. I have to say that they were very good, doing a mix of covers and some of their own material. The music was tremendously loud, but I really enjoyed it. I especially liked an original song they performed a couple of times entitled *The Rebel*. All in all, it turned out to be a great night.

As we walked back to 'The Majestic', Len said, "About what I said to yer earlier — about Mum I mean."

"You said that she was struggling a bit," I said.

Mint Vinyl

"More than a bit, Jack. If I'm honest see, I thought if we got the B&B going good again, she'd be ok yer know. It's like she's going through the motions."

"I know exactly where you're coming from, Len. You see it happened to my mum. When I was only young, Mum got the news one night via the police calling at the house. My dad had an accident on his motor bike. He was in hospital for the best part of two years. Well, my mum just fell apart — had a breakdown. Dad ended up in a wheelchair. Mum is still not herself, even to this day. So, I do know what it's like." We walked on, both in a sort of stunned silence.

Over the next few days, we chatted, but never like that night. I decided to stay for five days, which were extremely hectic in one way or another. Two nights were spent at 'The Hardrock,' where I saw live both Roxy Music and David Bowie as Ziggy Stardust. These two nights will stay with me for the rest of my life. Absolutely amazing — words simply fail. The rest of my time was spent replenishing my record stocks and getting lots of cash — not only for my records but also for my planned visit to a high-class jewellers in Manchester, as I wanted to purchase an engagement ring for April. I had gotten her ring size from Janette, and I planned to go to the jewellers on my last day.

Chapter 21

The Ring

The last day of my planned stay had arrived. After taking breakfast, I shared with Irene and Len my plans to buy the ring for April. Irene said, "That's just wonderful, Jack. I hope you find just the right one for her. All the best and congratulations."

"Yeah, me too, pal," said, Len. Feeling really good about my plans, I walked down the street to the main road and waited for a bus into the city centre. Once there I headed for Wellington Road to locate the jewellers: 'J. S. Franklin'. I entered the shop — a fairly large premises with lots of displays, about eight members of staff, and a dozen or so customers. I made my way to the display of engagement rings. I must say I was immediately spoiled for choice. This wasn't going to be as easy as I had thought. I must have been in there for around half an hour when one ring in particular caught my attention. I asked a member of staff if I could have a closer look.

"Certainly, sir," the young lady replied. She handed me the ring, and as soon as I was holding it I knew that it was

Mint Vinyl

the one for April. My full attention was on the ring, and at that precise moment I was completely oblivious to everything around me. Suddenly I was brought back to reality by shouting and the sound of smashing glass. Four men wearing balaclavas had entered the shop. Two were smashing the display cabinets with baseball bats, one was holding a sawn-off shotgun, and the other with what seemed to be a pistol. One of the men was shouting very loudly for us to get down on the floor, to stay down, and that no one needed to get hurt. Each of the men carried a large duffle bag, into which they were stuffing in lots of jewels. Both armed men kept their weapons trained on everyone. The man who had shouted previously spoke again to reiterate that as long as nobody did anything stupid, we would all be okay. In all the confusion and bewilderment of the raid I had forgotten all about the ring, which was no longer in my hand. I was prostrate, face down on the floor. I looked around and spotted the ring. I waited until I thought that the men weren't looking at me. I reached for the ring, but in doing so caught my palm on some glass, which was everywhere. I felt that the cut was bad—it certainly was hurting. However, I had managed to retrieve the ring unseen by the robbers. I lay there motionless for what seemed like an age but was in reality only a few minutes. As quickly as it had happened, it was all over.

Now we were left with the aftermath. I looked around me to see people physically showing the signs of the trauma

The Ring

that had just come upon us all. People were shaking, some sitting up with anguish on their faces, some holding their head in their hands, some comforting one another, and some sitting alone with tears streaking down their cheeks. The raid may have been over in one sense, but this would remain with this group of people for a long, long time. As for myself, I just sat on the floor simply unable to process the events of those few minutes. I was brought back to reality by the throbbing of my hand. I opened it up to reveal a bloodstained ring. The blood was flowing profusely from my hand. I took out my handkerchief from my pocket and wrapped it around my hand and raised my arm. Just then, the manager stood to his feet and asked everyone to try and remain as calm as possible and told us that that the police and ambulance were on their way. "Now do we have any injuries?" He asked.

I was loath to say anything, but a lady seated near to me said, "This man needs some attention." After this a young lady came to me with a first aid box. She removed my handkerchief and looked at my hand.

"That's rather deep. I think you will require stitches in that." After cleaning the wound, she bandaged it for me.

I in turn said, "Thank you very much." The police and ambulance arrived. Thankfully there were no serious injuries—not outwardly at least. People were treated for minor cuts and bruises, and I was advised to visit the hospital later that day. We were asked by the police to give statements,

Mint Vinyl

but I doubt that any would have proved that helpful. We saw no faces and the one man who did speak spoke very little. As for me, I made myself known to the manager of the store, showing him the ring, and stating that I would still like to purchase it.

He in turn said, "No problem at all, sir, we'll get it cleaned up for you. It will be ready tomorrow morning if that's acceptable."

"It is," I replied, "I'll call back in the morning."

It was only on my way back to 'The Majestic' that I began to realise just how much the events at the jewellers had shaken me up. On getting back, I related my tale to Irene and Len. They were more than a little surprised to hear my story. "You read about these sorts of things don't yer, but you never expect to be so close to it," Len remarked. They both asked how I was doing, and I tried to put on a brave face, but there was no doubt that the whole thing had really disturbed me.

After and early night I made my way back to the jewellers to collect the ring. When I arrived, the place was a hive of activity. There were some shop fitters there bringing in new cabinets and the whole place was once again clean and tidy. The manager himself, a Mr James Franklin, met me in the shop. He said, "So sorry about the events of yesterday, Mr..."

"Jack Roberts," I said.

The Ring

"Well, Mr Roberts, we have your ring ready for you as promised."

"Thank you so much, it means a lot to me."

"Now, sir, my colleague will take care of the details for you. Thank you for returning to us and thank you on behalf of Franklin's for your purchase. And once again, our sincere apologies for yesterday's events. Now, if you will excuse me, I must return to my work."

"Of course, sir, I understand. Thank you and goodbye." I said while shaking his hand.

Once I received the ring and settled my bill, I returned to 'The Majestic'. I had already packed my things and told Irene and Len that I would be leaving. After a tearful farewell I got a taxi to the station for my journey home. I had enjoyed my stay with Irene and Len – great people, I thought. I hoped that somehow Irene would one day feel better about things.

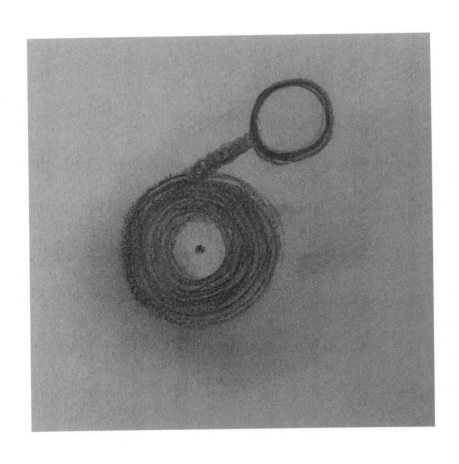

Chapter 22

Homeward Bound

On returning to Dansford station, I got a taxi back into town. After making my way onto the towpath, and once I was alone, I touched my specs and set the displays. I picked up my luggage and within seconds I was in my apartment. I had returned four days after I had left, simply because I was supposed to be away on business. After putting down my things I poured myself a large tot of rum and flopped down into my favourite chair. I began to think about all that had happened — my trip away from Dansford was, as always, a dangerous thing. By that I mean that going outside of the three-mile radius of the time device was always a great risk. I could travel outside of it, but I would have no means of getting back. What happened at Franklin's had really brought this into sharp focus for me. But then that's life, you never know what it's going to throw at you.

Still sitting in my chair, I suddenly became aware of my injured hand. It was swollen and had become quite painful. I felt I should go get my hand checked out. After spending a couple of hours in A&E, my hand was now stitched up

Mint Vinyl

and freshly bandaged. I had also been prescribed some antibiotics as my hand had become infected. After receiving a good telling off for not going for treatment sooner, I made my way home.

On returning I checked my phone. There were messages from Angela at the shop and also from Phillipa. After resting for a while, I decided to visit the shop. When I arrived, I could hardly believe my eyes. I saw a small group of people outside and noticed that the windows were both daubed with paint. Written on the small window was the message:

DON'T USE THIS SHOP HE'S A RUINER

And on the larger window:

BUSINESS RUINER.

There were three men outside handing out leaflets asking people not to use the shop. I went inside and spoke with Angela. "Mr Roberts, we're so glad you're here. It's been like this for a couple of days now," she said. "People are beginning to stay away."

"Okay, I'll see what I can do," I said. I went back outside to find Phillip Johnson and two helpers (if that's the right word), though I don't believe any of them were helping anyone really. I walked towards him and tried to speak.

"I told you it wasn't over, Roberts," he said.

Homeward Bound

"Please can we talk this thing over in a sensible manner?" I asked.

"Nothing to say to other than close your shops."

"Please let's try to settle this. Give me two minutes to speak to you at least."

"Make it snappy," he snarled. He really was very disagreeable.

"How about this," I said, "I will provide you with stock for your shop in an attempt to make it a level playing field. How about that?"

"Not interested. You don't get it do you? I don't like you—I detest you. Close your shops!"

I went back into the shop and spoke to the twins, apologising for what was happening and asking them to give me a few moments to think. I went into the back and made a call to Phillipa. "Hi, Phillipa, it's Jack," I said.

"Jack, where have you been?" she asked, "I've been calling you over and over."

"Sorry, I didn't have my phone."

"There's been trouble at the shops. I have tried to speak with Mr Johnson, but he won't listen to me."

"Me neither."

"I'll be there in about ten minutes."

"Okay, see you soon." Phillipa arrived and came into the stock room.

"You probably don't want to hear this, Jack, but you will have to call the police. This has to end." Reluctantly I agreed

Mint Vinyl

and made the call. The police arrived and took statements from the three, saying that they should leave immediately. One officer said to Mr Johnson that he was interfering with a legitimate business and then asked me if I wanted to have them arrested for damaging private property.

"There's no need for that, as long as you ask that they refrain from doing it again" I said, adding, "It's not fair on my staff or on my customers." They then received assurances that there would be no repeat of this. I thanked the officers as they left. All became quiet and the customers began to return. Going to the boot of my car, I took out half of the stock I had purchased in Manchester. I took them to the stock room, locked them in the large steel lockers, and gave the twins a list of the records. I then took the other half to my other shop.

Phillipa had said that she would call to mine tonight. I was looking forward to that. She really was a great asset to the business, and also a very good friend. The doorbell rang right on cue. I let Phillipa in, looking amazing as usual. I had prepared a meal for both of us and chosen a good bottle of wine. She quickly spotted my bandaged hand and wanted to know what had happened. After filling her in on all the details she said, "Jack, you get into the most amazing scrapes."

"It was really scary," I said, "I'm still having some flashbacks from it."

Homeward Bound

"It's a very risky business this time travel, Jack. I worry for you."

"You're not on your own there." We chatted more about Manchester, and I told her about April's ring. Of course, she wanted to see it. I gave her the box and after seeing the ring she declared, "Oh Jack, she'll love it. It's gorgeous. She's a lucky girl."

"I'm a lucky man to have met her." Eventually the conversation turned to the events of earlier in the day.

Phillipa said, "I think that will be an end to it now."

"I sincerely hope so," I said. But in my heart of hearts, I couldn't help but think that this guy hadn't finished yet. The last thing I wanted was for Phillipa to be worried about all of this. But it just seemed that everything I did brought about trouble for my dearest friends. After a wonderful evening together Phillipa made a call to her chauffer. Ten minutes later, he rang the doorbell. Phillipa kissed me on the cheek and thanked me for the evening.

"I will give you a call," she said, before she was off into the night.

I was hoping for a good night's sleep, but I didn't get one. I kept having dreams about the jewel raid and about Phillip Johnson. I rose early and went through my daily routine. I had decided to visit Tony, so made all the preparations for a visit. Soon enough I was on the towpath. I had brought my record case along with me as I planned to pick up some important albums that Tony had got for me. It was a nice bright day. As I walked along I began to forget my troubles, at least for a few moments. Sure enough, after a few minutes they all tumbled in on me again. I had been unable to shake of the feeling I had — that in the pursuit of my dreams I had brought nothing but unhappiness to all of my friends. When I was nearing Tony's, I remembered that I had brought the engagement ring to show Tony, as well as a small gift for Lucy from Manchester, a keyring in the shape of an LP record that I thought she would really like. Reaching the shop, I went in to see Lucy serving a customer and two or three other customers browsing the records. Lucy looked up as I entered and gave me a big beaming smile. When the customer had left Lucy said, "Lookin' for Dad?"

"Yes," I said, "is he in the back?"

"He's just popped into town for a few things. Only been gone about ten minutes."

"Okay, I just wanted to see him about the imports. Also, I have a small gift for you."

"What is it, Uncle Jack?" she asked excitedly. I felt inside my pocket and pulled out my keys, glasses case, and also at last Lucy's gift. She took hold of it and said, "Thanks, Uncle Jack, it's fab."

"Glad you like it." I then took the ring from my pocket and said, "Lucy, I would like you to look at this. It's for April." She opened the box and her eyes lit up.

"Wow, that's fabulous," she said, "you'll be able to knock her down with a feather when she sees this."

Homeward Bound

"Thanks, I was bowled over by it too. Anyway, Lucy love, I'll leave you to your customers. Tell Dad I'll call back later."

"Okay, Uncle Jack... will do. See you later."

I left the shop intending to just take a stroll, but as I got outside I was startled by a loud voice shouting, "Roberts, I want you!" I looked up to see Kevin Wilson coming towards me. *I don't like the look of this*, I thought. I began to walk quickly down Hunt Street with Wilson still following me and shouting. My only thought was of escaping this man, so I began running. Soon I was on Thomas Street, after which I headed down the first street on the left. I glanced over my shoulder to see that he was hot on my heels. I began to quicken my pace, turning first right then left in a desperate effort to get away. But he was keeping pace with me. After darting down another street, I came onto what I recognised as Princess Street. Suddenly a thought flashed into my mind. Just further down the street was an indoor market. *I'll make a dash for it in there*, I thought, *I'll be able to lose him in the crowd*. Even though there were lots of people on the streets, everyone seemed far too busy to notice what was going on with me. Glancing back once more, I saw that Wilson was still with me. *He moves well for a big man*, I thought. I reached the doors and pushed them open. Entering the market, I found lots more people inside. I was now really beginning to tire, feeling out of breath. Progress inside the marked was much more difficult, the only

Mint Vinyl

consolation being that it was the same for Wilson. There does seem to be an unwritten law that says whatever direction you are going, everyone else is going opposite to you. I weaved in and out of the crowds of people, going in between the many stalls any time there was a gap. Try as I may I could still hear him shouting my name. Finally, I realised that this was getting me nowhere. I couldn't shake him off. *It's like wading through treacle in here*, I thought.

I spotted an exit and headed for it. Pushing the door open, I ran for all I was worth down the street and the next one too. Wilson was now a little ways back on me. I quickly ran down the next street, turned on my right, and came to a stop. It was then that I thought the unthinkable. *I'll have to use the EDS.* I hoped that I would never have occasion to use it. Uncle George had explained the EDS (Emergency Displacement System) in his letter, writing:

> *Jack my boy, only use this if in dire circumstances.*

What I had to do was remove my specs and place them into my case and close the lid.

> *You will be thrust back to your time Jack, and I do mean thrust. The action knocked me off my feet for days.*

I felt that it was now or never. Reaching into my pocket for the case, I was horrified to find that it was no longer there.

Homeward Bound

My mind raced back to earlier — I had taken it out at Tony's. Desperation filled my very being. Once more I ran down another street, then that was it. I could go no further. I was bent almost double, with my back against a wall. Gasping for breath and holding my knees, all of my body seemed to be aching. I was feeling dizzy thinking, *Well this is it, I can't go on, so what will be will be*, when suddenly a hand came upon my shoulder. My eyes were closed, and my heart was pounding like it was going to come out of my chest, when I heard a voice say, "Listen, Jack, what are you doing here?" I can't begin to explain the feelings that rushed throughout my body at that moment. At first I was so out of breath I found myself unable to speak.

Eventually I pulled myself upright, and gripping Tony by his shoulder I said, "Thanks, Tony."

"For what? I haven't done anything," he said.

"So glad to see you that's all." I was still rather shaky, but we began to make our way back to Tony's shop. On the way I related to him about my little adventure so to speak.

"Listen, wonder what that was about," he said.

"I haven't got a Scooby," I replied. Tony looked at me bewildered. "Sorry, mate, sometimes I just forget myself, what I mean is I have no clue as to why he wanted me." We walked on still chatting until we reached the shop. When we got in I said to Lucy, "Did you find my specs case anywhere, Lucy dear?"

"Yes, after you left," she answered, "you put it down on the counter." She then handed the case to me. I had asked Tony to not mention my incident and he had agreed. I had no desire to upset anyone else with my troubles.

Taking Tony to one side I said to him, "Still feeling shaken from the encounter, going home to rest and think things over, got an awful lot on my mind at the moment. See you in a couple of days."

"Listen, Jack, take it easy right!" he said, with a hand on each shoulder, looking me straight in the eyes. "Try not to worry so much."

"Okay, see you soon my friend." I left the shop and, after making my way to the towpath, I once again set the displays and returned back home.

Chapter 23

Whatever

I slumped into my chair, my mind racing with many thoughts about my run-in with Wilson and what had happened in Manchester. Despite my best efforts, I couldn't remove these thoughts from my mind — thoughts that everything I did just brought trouble for me, and everyone concerned with me. Two days passed in this way. I was getting little sleep, and I was trying to do my best, but it wasn't happening. For the most part I just sat in my pyjamas and dressing gown. I was also quite weak from not eating much. As I was sitting in my chair I suddenly made a conscious decision that this needed to stop — all this wallowing in self-pity. *It's not just about me*, I told myself. I went for a shower and a shave and got dressed for the sixties to see Tony to see if together we can be cheered.

I made all the preparations to arrive two days after my last visit. Soon enough I was walking down the towpath towards Tony's. It was around 10:30am — a sunny day at that moment. I was feeling brighter, but that was about to change. As I got within sight of the shop I saw Tony outside.

Mint Vinyl

He looked to be hammering nails into boards over some of the windows. I quickened my steps and shouted to Tony, "What's going on, Tony? What's happened?"

"It's Rossi," said Tony, "that's what's happened." Tony beckoned me inside. What a mess it was—racks overturned, and records strewn all over.

"When did this all happen, Tony?"

"Earlier this morning two men walked into the shop. One says, 'Mr Hibbert, is it?' I said, 'That's right, and you are?' He says, 'Never mind that, is your protection insurance up to date?' Then one of them grabs me, holding me against the wall, while the other does this. On their way out they smash two of the windows. I was just boarding them up when you came. Listen, it's really shaken Lucy up. Can you lock the door, Jack, and turn the sign to closed? Must go to see how Lucy is."

"Of course, go to her." I did as Tony had asked and then began trying to tidy things up. Presently, Tony and Lucy came in from the back. Lucy was visibly shaken and still crying. Tony was livid but was trying to keep a lid on it.

Lucy cuddled me round my waist saying, "Uncle Jack, it was awful—I was so scared."

"I know sweetheart," I said, "but try not to think about it too much." She went back to her dad, who suggested that she try and get some rest. Reluctantly she went up to bed. Meanwhile, Tony and I set about the task of clearing up the mess.

Whatever

Around lunchtime we heard a knocking at the door. I opened up to find it was Dave Rossi stood there. He said, "Well, well, if it's not Jack or whatever your name is." Tony joined me at the door. Rossi then said, "This is a bit of a mess, isn't it?"

Tony responded, "Why are you here, Rossi?"

"Just a courtesy call, Mr Hibbert—reminding you that this sort of thing doesn't happen when you have protection insurance!" Tony would have liked to have a swing at him, but I positioned myself between them.

I then said, "Think you should leave now."

"Okay," said Rossi, "but just consider my offer. All of this could go away. See you now." He then turned and left. I knew that Tony would never make a deal with Dave Rossi, but in that moment, I made a conscious decision to do that very thing before I left for home. I would never tell Tony of my plans however, but I reasoned that it was the only way for Tony and his family to be free of this awful situation that I thought rested squarely on my shoulders. We carried on clearing up, putting everything back in its place until Janette came home from work. Tony told her what happened, and she was of course very upset by it all.

I tried to lighten the mood by saying, "We'll think of something to sort this whole mess out."

Then Tony said, "Listen, Jack, you must stay for your tea."

"Okay then," I replied, "if it's no trouble."

Mint Vinyl

Janette prepared a meal, which we shared, and began to feel a little better about things. I looked at the clock and said, "Look at the time, it's after ten. I'd better get going."

"No way you're going anywhere at this time," said Tony, "you can stay in the spare room." After chatting some more, Tony showed me the spare room. Taking off my clothes, I got into bed and tried to get some sleep, but for a long period, sleep evaded me. Just too much going on in my mind.

After taking breakfast with the family, I told them that I would really have to leave, but that I would return again soon. Leaving Tony's, I made my way to the bank and made a withdrawal. Then I made my way to Dave Rossi's betting shop. When I entered, Mark Stanley immediately shouted into the back, "You might want to come to the front, boss!"

Rossi made his way in growling, "What is it?" Seeing me he looked, shall we say, something less that happy. "You don't come in here!" Dave was very agitated.

I then said, "Keep calm, Dave, I'm here to talk business."

"In the back," he barked. To cut a long story short, I made a deal with the devil, so to speak.

Paying what he wanted, I asked, "Now, all this will stop yes?"

"You have my word," he replied. I wasn't actually filled with confidence at Dave's remark but had little choice but to accept it. Before I left, Dave handed me a small notebook for my payments. "So, we know where we're up to," he added. Dave's last words to me were, "You play ball with me, and I'll play ball with you." I felt some kind of relief that Tony and his family would be okay now but couldn't help but think that I had opened myself up to lots of bad things now that Dave had me where he wanted me. But all this was consoled by the fact that I would get the money for his protection insurance from other bookmakers. I also had a real propensity for believing that people who deserved their comeuppance would one day get it — I felt for certain that Mr Dave Rossi would get his one day.

Arriving back at my apartment, and having just gone into the lounge, my phone started to ring. I picked it up and saw that it was Phillipa. I answered saying, "Hi, Phillipa, what's new?"

Her voice sounded stressed as she said, "Jack, oh Jack, I've been trying to reach you. It's your mum — she's been taken ill." Almost immediately, a kind of dark cloud seemed to cover me, and I thought, *Whatever next?*

I stood speechless, rooted to the spot, when Phillipa's voice said, "Jack, are you still there, my love?"

"Yes, I'm here. I have to go to her." I knew that Mum had been to visit a friend in London — Ruth Simpson is the lady's name — she used to live two doors down from Mum when she lived at home. "Phillipa, I'll get to Manchester, then catch another train to London."

"There's no way I'll let you go alone. I'm coming too." Fifteen minutes later, she was ringing my doorbell. In that time, I had packed a bag with a few things, and I was ready to go. When I answered the door, she threw her arms around me. "Jack my sweet, I'm so very sorry for you."

I simply said, "Thank you."

"My chauffer will drive us to Manchester to get the train."

I remember virtually nothing of our journey there. We sat in the back, Phillipa holding my hand, squeezing it now and then. There was no conversation, just glances to one another. We arrived at Manchester Piccadilly station and Phillipa bought two return tickets to Euston station. We had just twenty minutes to wait, after which we boarded the train and were on our way. I was feeling somehow numb towards everything. I couldn't seem to think straight. When I could focus on my thoughts, they were dark and depressing. I must have been obvious to Phillipa that I was not, shall we say, coping very well. "Jack my sweet," she said, "please try to talk to me. I want to be here for you." Even in the midst of all this terrible anguish, her wonderful demeanour shone through.

"I know you do," I said, "it's just hit me so hard. Everything seems to be going wrong and it all seems to point to me."

"I'm sure that's not true."

"My mum had it so hard you know. Losing my dad twice really — once with the accident, and then with the heart attack. Did I ever tell you that they were childhood sweethearts — totally inseparable. Both loved motorbikes, going all over together on Dad's second-hand bike. And then, in a very real sense, she also lost me—for all of my childhood at least anyway."

"Yes, I see it must have been so very difficult for her."

"She never really got over it you know." The conversation stopped. I gazed out the window at the passing countryside, with all kinds of memories coming and going through my mind.

Once there, we got a cab to the hospital. We went in and asked where Mum was, after which we were directed to a small ward and informed that Mum had suffered a bad stroke and was unconscious. We went in and there she was. *She looks terrible*, I thought to myself. We sat on either side of her bed, and I held her hand. She seemed so lifeless lying there. Once again, my thoughts raced, *Is this where my dreams have led me?* We were there for about an hour before I suggested to Phillipa that we find somewhere to stay. She replied, "Okay then, let's do that."

We called a cab back into the city and checked into a motel. I suggested she stay in the motel for a while to try and get some rest. "I'll go back," I said, "join me later." I just put my bag into my room and returned to the hospital. I was awoken by Phillipa several hours later that day, still holding Mum's hand. The doctor suggested that we come back in the morning, to which I reluctantly agreed. I left my mobile number with the hospital, saying, "Call me if there are any developments."

Mint Vinyl

After being there for two days I said to Phillipa, "I feel so helpless. I don't feel that we are accomplishing anything by being here. She doesn't know I'm here. I feel we should go back home."

"If that's what you want, Jack, I'm with you." Phillipa called her chauffer so that he could be waiting for us in Manchester. During the journey back, I convinced myself that I needed to go away somewhere—away from it all. I spoke to Phillipa about it, and she said, "Do you really think it wise? You are in a fragile state, Jack, and I'm worried for you."

"I have to say this to you. I feel that I'm stood on the edge of a gaping black hole, about to fall in and be swallowed up." This did nothing to dispel her fears for me.

"Where will you go?" she asked. It's then that I told her of a plan to visit a place called Castle Combe in Wiltshire. I had found it in an old book in a charity shop and found myself captivated by it. Obviously, it would have been better under different circumstances. "I can't talk you out of it?" she said.

"No, please don't worry. Everything will be fine. I just need time to think away from everything. Please will you look after things for me."

"Yes of course," she said, giving me a smile. After dropping me off back at my apartment she got out with me. Giving me a hug and kissing me on the cheek, she whispered to me, even lower than normal, "Please be safe, Jack."

Whatever

"I promise that I will," I replied. I waved as she got back into the car and left. Going in, I immediately put my plan into action, doing everything necessary for my trip. I would leave the following day, but there was one thing I omitted to say to Phillipa—my trip would be to 1933. Well, I didn't want to alarm her anymore that she was already.

Chapter 24

A Planned Trip

I awoke early, having set my alarm for 4:30am, still feeling very depressed. I followed my daily routine after taking breakfast, but in reality, more of it was wasted than eaten. Going into the bedroom, I checked through the bag I'd packed for taking with me. I took out a suit from the wardrobe, laying it on the bed. I then put on a shirt, a tie I had chosen, and then the suit, all of which would fit in with the time period I had chosen. Standing in the mirror and looking at myself, I thought, *Uncle George would be proud of my attire*. My plan was to take a taxi to Dansford station, then on by train to Manchester. I had thought to break up my journey upon reaching London, reasoning that it would probably be quite late by the time I expected to arrive — travel in that time not being what it is today.

All was going well and according to plan until I arrived in Manchester. There had been only a small number of passengers on the train to Manchester, and not many of them spoke to me. However, the LMS train to London was a very different matter. There were six people in my coach, five be-

Mint Vinyl

sides me. They all seemed rather chirpy and chatty, apart from me. When spoken to of course I showed people the common courtesy of replying, but, in all honesty, it was the last thing I wanted to do. This must sound awful, but I found the journey rather irksome. I wasn't any fault of my fellow travellers, just myself and my despairing feelings.

Eventually we reached our destination. As I was leaving the platform, I asked the ticket collector if he could recommend a good small hotel nearby. "Sure thing, guv," he said, "just go to the taxi rank and ask for 'The Regent' on Jubilee Road."

"Thanks so much," I replied.

"All part of the service, guv. Good evening to ya." Following his instructions, I arrived at 'The Regent'. I asked for bed and breakfast, one night only. I managed to get about three hours sleep I would say. After breakfast and paying the bill, the porter called a cab for me to go back to the station. This time I would be travelling on the GWR to Bath. I purchased my ticket and, having a wait of half an hour before my train would be leaving, I waited on a bench near platform seven holding a newspaper I had purchased. I say holding, because I had little interest in reading, but thought it may dissuade passengers from engaging me in conversation. That goes some way in summing up how bad I was feeling at that moment.

Once we arrived at Bath, something occurred that I hadn't anticipated. Getting off the train, I spoke to the por-

A Planned Trip

ter to ask about getting into the village, which I knew to be about twelve miles outside bath. The problem I had was one of communication. It sounded to me as if he was saying, 'Ee finda drive.' It seems that in the local dialect, people had this habit of adding letters to words, and also missing them out altogether. I didn't know what he was saying to me. Fortunately, a fellow passenger was able to help me. He raised his hat and said, "Follow me." We left the station and outside were a couple of horse and carriages. "The porter was saying, 'you need to find a driver.'" Thanking the man for his help and climbing in, we set off for the village. I paid the driver and walked down a narrow lane until I reached a pub called the 'Red Lion'. It was early evening by now, and there were quite a few people in there.

I went up to the bar and asked the landlord, "Excuse me, sir, do you have any rooms available?" He looked at me and replied in a very broad dialect. I had no idea what he was saying.

Just as I was thinking that the situation was hopeless, a man walked to the bar and said, "There are no rooms left. They only have two, and they are both taken."

He told me his name was John, to which I said, "Good to meet you. My name is Jack. Jack Roberts." I then asked him, "Are there any more places to stay?"

"No, but you can stay with me and the wife and my young lad."

"I couldn't presume on you like that."

Mint Vinyl

"That's that then, ee can follow me then." Off we went back down the lane until we reached John's cottage. We entered to see his wife there. "This be Jack," said John, "Jack, this be my wife, Mary."

"Very pleased to meet you, Mary," I said.

"Where be Billy, my lovely?" asked John.

"Bringing more wood fawt fire," she replied.

"Sit thee down, Jack, and mack theeself at home." I was to find out later that John and his family had worked with people from the Northwest of England, so they spoke to me that way, which was to be invaluable to me during my stay. Presently, young Billy came in with some firewood, as Mary was doing some baking. Billy was about seven—a strong lively boy.

He said to me, "Pleased to meet ee, Mister Jack." When he spoke, he was very direct and somewhat disarming, saying to me, "Mister Jack, will ee be my friend?"

"Of course, Billy," I said. We had only just met, but there already seemed to be something between us. I remember thinking it quite strange. We spoke for a while about my visit to the village. I tried to give away as little detail as possible. Later, John showed me my room.

Surprisingly, I slept well—it must have been my long journey. After waking, I washed and changed, and went into the kitchen to see Mary and young Billy in there. She smiled and said to me, "Sit ee down. Have some breakfast." She put some porridge into a bowl for me and started to

A Planned Trip

make some toast over the fire. It was the bread that she was making yesterday. Feeling hungry, I quickly ate my porridge and the toast, both of which tasted so good. They were washed down with a strong mug of tea.

Billy had been reading a book, but then said to me, "Will ee come out today wi me, Mister Jack?"

"Billy, ee must leave Jack today to himself," said Mary. Billy seemed quite disappointed but returned to his book.

"Where's John?" I asked.

"Ee be in his workshop out back," she said, pointing at the door. I went to the door through into a lean-to building. John was in there busy working shaping wood with a sharp tool. He had pieces of wood clamped down in a sort of frame, the wood held in place by pressing down on a large foot pedal. He made the work look very easy. I was later to find out that John made furniture.

"Sorry for not being very good company last night," I said.

"That bee alright. Ee must have been tired." After thanking him once more for the hospitality, and just as I turned to leave, he said, "Ee can stay has long has ee likes thi knows."

I told Mary that I was going for a walk and made my way outside. Going down the lane past the market cross and out into the fields, I spotted young Billy with several other kids. They ran up and down, having races with hoops propelled with a wooden stick—back and forth they ran. They were

Mint Vinyl

having great fun. Their shouting and laughter seemed to fill the air. As I walked I began to see some of the beauty of the place. Once out into the fields, I lay down on my back, having to shield my eyes from the sun. It was turning into a wonderful day — weatherwise at least. I closed my eyes to what seemed like total darkness. All the grief and anguish swept over me. I thought of Mum, of Uncle George, Auntie Suzanne, and of all that I knew swirling inside my head. Tears flowed — I sobbed for a long time, my eyes red and swollen. Even as I lay in the midst of this beauty, all seemed to be lost in darkness. Everything had gone wrong. It was all down to the pursuit of my dreams. That's how it seemed to me.

After several hours, I picked myself up and started to walk back to the village. As I got near to the river, I stopped and washed my face. I made it back to the cottage, and saw the children were gone now. I knocked and walked in. Mary, John, and Billy were having dinner — what I would call lunch. Mary said, "Wash up, Jack, and sit ee down." She gave me a bowl of stew and some home baked bread.

Over the coming days my life was to change so dramatically because of these people. I went fishing with Billy. He was so bright that young lad, so full of life. He would tell me the names of all the trees and plants he saw on our trips and would point out animal tracks. He was disarming — I was in awe of this young boy. Slowly my depression was lifting from me. I watched John in his workshop, and we

A Planned Trip

laughed when he invited me to try to do things — it was hilarious. John also had a rod lathe, a springy branch with rope to make the lathe turn via a foot pedal. I would spend hours with him just watching as he produced parts for his furniture. John was a brilliant craftsman. As I watched the interaction between these three and towards others, my whole attitude changed. Here were people who in essence had very little but were prepared to share that with everyone. I was so moved by them and my surroundings.

I felt so much better and began to see this place for what it was. Down by the lane ran the river, with rows of cottages on both sides, stone cottages with stone roofs — they were breathtaking. I had never been to such a beautiful place — I just drank it all in.

After two glorious weeks of wonderful sunshine, with the odd spot of rain, it was time for me to leave. I packed and told John and Mary that I would leave the next morning. "We'll all be sad to see ee go, Jack," said John.

"You will never know how much I will miss you all," I said. "John, you and your family and this place have given me back my life."

"Well thank ee, but we have done nothing." Billy was out playing when it was time for me to leave.

After a tearful farewell with John and Mary, Billy came running up to me, jumping into my arms saying, "Mister Jack, when ee first came ee was very sad. Now ee happy. I love ee, Mister Jack." Tears flowed down my cheeks.

Mint Vinyl

"Love you too, Billy," I said, holding him close. It was now time to leave. driver had arrived to take me to the station. Saying farewell to John, Mary, and Billy, and this idyllic place, was one of the hardest things I've ever had to do.

My journey back was very different than before. I was now a changed man. I was now more than willing to meet with people on my journey home. Between conversations with people, I made plans in my mind as to what needed to be done. I was thinking clearly now, and everything seemed to be clicking into place.

Chapter 25

The Future

I returned back to my own time a couple of days after I had left. Checking my phone, I found some messages from Phillipa asking how I was doing, adding that there had been no other word concerning Mum. I contacted the hospital, being told that she was stable but no change. I began to write down plans for the future, after which I called Phillipa. I arranged to meet with her at 'The Lantern' that evening. I arrived to see that bright sign which was as recognisable to its clientele as the golden arches are to others. As always, Phillipa arrived on time. As soon as she saw me, she remarked, "You look much better, Jack."

I thanked her and said, "I do. I'm a changed man."

"It's so good to have the old Jack back."

After a lovely meal I told her my decision, "I'm going to wind everything up and return to sixty-three to live one life with April." I related to her how I had rushed headlong into the pursuit of my dreams with very little thought of anything else. I posed to her a question, and to myself I suppose — had I really achieved anything? I had brought

Mint Vinyl

some joy to some, I had probably caused sales to increase in various years, and I had certainly put many more mint condition albums into circulation, but had it been the right thing to do? I just didn't know. She was very understanding about it all.

"Jack my dear," she said, "as long as you're happy, that's all that matters to me."

I then said, "I have a cheque for your initial investment plus interest." She just smiled, thanked me, and kissed me on the cheek.

"Oh, Jack, always so sweet." We finalised the details together, after which she left. We had decided to meet again tomorrow at my first shop around closing time.

The next morning, I called to both the shops, asking them all to meet up after closing time at my first store. Phillipa and I arrived almost together. We entered the shop to see everyone present. I started by saying that I have called them together for a special announcement. I said, "Due to certain circumstances in my life, I have decided to close both my shops this coming Friday. Now I want to stress this has no bearing on any of you. You have all been brilliant. I couldn't have done it without you. Now I have for you each an envelope containing two week's holiday pay plus a redundancy package that I hope will be adequate. Now do you have any questions?"

The Future

Angela said, "Not as such, just a great big thanks for everything you've done. It's been brilliant working here for you."

All the others joined in, saying, "Yes, that's right, Mr Roberts."

"Please call me Jack."

"Okay," they said, "just this once." I also told them that I had provided a good reference for them all, adding that I thought they would have no trouble finding employment. It was in some ways a very sad day, but I was looking to the future now. I then told Phillipa that I would see her before leaving, to finalise some things. I would call her the next morning to arrange our meeting. I began to

After she left, I headed off back to my apartment. I listened to some music on my record player, poured myself some rum, and settled into my chair, thinking over all that needed to be done tomorrow. *It's going to be a big day*, I thought, *a great day*. I began to feel relaxed and found myself starting to nod off. I thought to myself, *This is the best I have felt in what must be months*. I went to bed and slept soundly.

Glancing at my bedside table, the clock read 7:20am. I arose, showered, shaved, and dressed ready for the day. After breakfast, I called Phillipa and arranged to meet at the café we went to once before. I made sure I was there early. "Hi, Jack," she said, as she came over to the table. I rose from my seat and kissed her on the cheek. "I can't get over the transformation," she said, "you just look so well, Jack." We

Mint Vinyl

both sat and I told her about my visit to 1933 and about Jack, Mary, and Billy—how I was simply humbled by their lives, and how the trip had brought me to my senses. I asked Phillipa if she would oversee the closing of the shops with me. "Of course, Jack my love," she said, "anything you need just ask. I'm here for you."

I then said, "I plan to visit Tony and his family, also to go and propose to April."

"All will go well, Jack. She'll say yes."

"After that I will return to sort everything out with your help."

"Look forward to seeing you then, my love. One more thing before you go, Jack. April, she's a very lucky girl."

I blushed up and quickly said, "See you soon." By this time, we were just in the doorway of the café. She waved and off she went.

I returned home and prepared to visit Tony. I took the ring with me, as well as this journal I have been writing and drawing in. I have mentioned it to Tony and Janette on several occasions, saying that they will know more about my other life when they read it through. Perhaps there is a future in the past.

The Future

The shop door opened, and Jack walked in with a smile from ear to ear. "Hi, Tony. Hi, Lucy," he said.

"So good to see you, Uncle Jack," said Lucy.

"Listen, pal, so good to see you looking so well. You really do look great."

"I feel it too."

"Are you off to see April then?"

"Yes I'm both excited and also extremely nervous."

"Listen, don't worry. She'll say yes in a flash."

"Before I go, this is for you all to read. Well, here I go, wish me Luck."

"You won't need it," we said in unison.

I walked out of the door with Jack and shook his hand saying, "See you in a bit."

Jack went to cross the road. Halfway across a car came from nowhere. The next thing I knew there was a terrible thud, and Jack was thrown up into the air. The car sped off and Jack lay motionless in the road. Lucy *ran out to him, and I called for an ambulance and the police. The ambulance arrived and took Jack to the local hospital. I asked Lucy to tell her mum and April what had happened, and I went with Jack to the hospital. Afterwards I was joined by Lucy, Janette, and April. Finally, a doctor came in to tell us about Jack.*

He said, "Mr Roberts is stable now, but has suffered very serious injuries." We were all very upset and concerned. However, the doctor told us that Jack needed to rest, and that it might be better if we returned home, as there was nothing we could do. Reluctantly we left, after I gave the hospital the shop telephone number. We returned the next day, only to be told that Jack was in a coma.

Over a period of six weeks, we have visited as much as we can. I have decided to carry on writing this in Jack's journal so that he will know what has happened when he is well again. During one of our visits, I said to the consultant in charge, "He will get better won't he?"

"Well, Mr Hibbert," he said, "my team and I will do all in our power to bring about a full recovery for Mr Roberts. But all I can say for certain is only time will tell.

Printed in Great Britain
by Amazon